IN SEAR

LOVE

LIFE SOMETIMES CAN BE CONFUSING

This is a work of fiction. Names, character, places and incidents are either the product of the author's imagination or are used fictitiously, and any resemblance to actual persons, living or dead, business establishments, events or locales is entirely coincidental.

Table of Contents

4

CHAPTER 1

The USS Jacob Hull's bobtail refit at Naval Station Mayport was being assisted by the Jacksonville Shipyard, and the Chief Engineer, Chief Machinery Repairman, Executive Officer, and project manager were there to help. They all sadly observed the wreckage of the starboard steering engine control system. The switchboard and the electric motor that powered the steering engine were also destroyed, and the hydraulic lines and hydraulic pump had suffered damage. The steering engine was essential for the destroyer to be able to depart port.

The project manager eventually said, "Don't look to us for replacement components. The design is older than that, and that gear was 20 years old. To obtain them, you'll probably need to steal a vessel in Beaumont's reserve fleet.

Similar to how Jeeves coughed to draw Haley Wooster's attention, the Chief Eng heard his chief cough. To the XO, he raised an eyebrow.

The Chief Engineer said, "Sir, there's only one man for this task.

The XO concurred, "You're correct. The Officer of the Deck was keeping watch in port on the quarterdeck, so he moved to the sound-powered phone, flipped a switch to summon him there, and started cranking. He said, "Call the First Lieutenant to the steering engine room."

The project manager climbed the staircase to the main deck and remarked, "I'll leave you to it. He felt there would be a display of fireworks and didn't want to be a part of it.

Although there had been no announcement over the ship's public address system, a tall, lean officer with blonde hair slid into the steering engine flat a minute later wearing non-standard weather-bleached khaki coveralls with railroad tracks on the collar points, a Surface Warfare Officer's badge over the left pocket, and an equally non-standard khaki baseball cap with a Navy officer's cap insignia pinned to the front on his head.

You called, sir?" he inquired.

The Chief Engineer greeted Mr. Jadens in the morning as the "pit boss," the senior enlisted engineer, winced. The ChEng was a fan of the Mission: Impossible television series and had a tendency of giving briefings for challenging assignments as if he were the voice on the tape recorder Jim Phelps would occasionally find in strange places and use to direct him on his missions. "You are looking at a dead hydraulic pump and control system for the starboard steering engine. We have to stay at the dock till the steering engine is working because we have to take the Hull out for speed testing in three days. The shipyard claims that they are out of spare parts.

Should you want to accept it, your task is to track down the required components, collect them, and bring them back so that the steering may be fixed by that time. The Captain will, of course, deny any knowledge of your acts if you are discovered or taken into custody. Happy hunting, Wally.

Jadens remarked, "You're a hilarious, funny man, sir.

The XO questioned, "Wally, are you doing anything that can't wait?

"No." He gave it some thinking. "May I choose my own men?"

The Executive Officer said, "Take anybody you need." Just keep me informed so I can hold you accountable or, if necessary, get you out of trouble.

Wally glanced to the Chief, who had been calmly observing all of this. "Chief, let's go for a walk together. By your permission, sir? He and the Pit Boss walked out of the room without waiting for a response. They were looked after by the ChEng and XO.

The engineer eventually said, "Sending those two to obtain spares is like ordering Steven Freeman and Sir Francis Benson to enter the King of Spain's coffers and assist themselves.

"Imagine witnessing a female diver perform an inward back layout of one and a half off the 10 meter platform. Don't ask her how; simply acknowledge the talent at work. Jadens and Chief Flores will be able to obtain the components if anybody can so that we don't miss our test date.

The Chief handed the lieutenant one of the two cups of coffee before moving forward and disappearing inside the ship's office. They sipped the powerful brew as they leaned over the railing below the bridge to watch the water. "Just how horrible is it?" Jaden enquired.

"Rather than trying to improve current system, it would be simpler to design a brand-new one."

While we still had oil-fired carriers, weren't you stationed here, Patch?

"Yeah. I was on the final trip of the vintage O'Brien before she was retired. Back then, Edward the Tin Can Killer was escorted by an entire squadron of Spruances. Wally, why?

The loggies never clear up the warehouses, and you snipes did a lot of your own maintenance. Let's go see now.

The two grabbed the truck allocated to the Hull and drove to the supply depot, stopping just long enough to have the ship's yeoman print out the appropriate papers after ordering him to add "or equivalent" to the parts procurement form. To speak with the storekeepers, they entered the office. Lt. Jadens made a point to see the Officer in Charge and express his condolences. Through the locked door, which suddenly opened, he could hear shouting.

Two splashes of color on her high cheekbones and a long-legged, auburn-haired woman in a miniskirt and heels ran by him. She had a wasp waist and high-set boobs that appeared larger than they actually were. She had bright green eyes that flashed, the rare shade of white skin that is only seen on true redheads, and what appeared to be a temper to match the hair. Before entering the outside door and slamming it behind her, she swept an approving glance over him, paused for a brief moment, raised an eyebrow, and gave him a little wink. The OIC had storm clouds covering his face as he stood at the doorway.

"Worst time?" Wally queried.

CHAPTER 2

Waving him inside the office, the lieutenant with the Supply Corps' "pork chop" on his left collar point complained, "No... no, not really." Jadens, what can the Supply Corps accomplish for the Hull today?

"The yardbirds say they don't have the components to replace the steering engine, which broke down. I intended to speak with you. I wonder whether the engineering spares for the Spruances are still in storage as my Chief mentioned that they were originally kept in the depot.

Because they were all destroyed, I scoff at the idea, but weirder things have happened. Consider one of my strikers to be your local guide. You could be fortunate. To be safe, he grabbed a duplicate of the request the yeoman had created.

They emerged from the building carrying a young farm guy just out of boot camp who was off on his first duty. The sailor led them to a warehouse that appeared to have been abandoned for some time. Pallets of greasy parts for different ship engineering systems were illuminated by lights that flared into existence. The Chief found what he was seeking for after 30 minutes.

This is adequate, he murmured. "Wally, the electric motor, the control system, and the pump can all be rebuilt if necessary. In actuality, there are two of them present, fully. According to the tags, they left the old Moosbrugger on a DX.

Grab them both, Patch," Jadens commanded. "There can never be too many spares. Combine and contrast, and if we have the time, we'll also update the port set. little hassle in that manner. He questioned the seaman, "Is there a forklift in here?"

I noticed one beside the large doors, but I have no idea how to operate it, sir.

"Thankfully, I do. I'll fetch the hyster, you bring the truck here.

The forklift was driven back to its parking spot by Jadens after the two pallets had been loaded into the truck, and the Chief and the youngster slowly followed.

The sailor timidly said, "Sir, may I ask you something?"

Chief rather than sir.

'You've finished boot camp now, young man. Sir is Wally, not me. What are you considering?

Isn't it odd, si — Chief, that an officer would operate a forklift while addressing you by your nickname?

"Yeah, but Mr. Jadens isn't your standard policeman. I served as his engineer while he was in charge of an outdated Stenka-class patrol boat in Brazil, where he was assisting the Brazilian Navy with a small issue they had in the Amazon a few years prior. It matters when you've been shot at collectively. He nicknames me "Patch" since I'm adept at repairing things using non-standard components so they function better than they did before. He follows the rules only when it is convenient; that is how things are done in the Brown Water Navy, where he has spent the most of his career.

"Stenka has a Russian-sounding name."

"It is."

"I had no idea the Navy possessed any ships from Russia,"

You still don't know a lot about the Navy, young man. But I'll tell you this: having an officer like Wally Gator in charge will make you feel really comfortable when the shots start flying.

Flores retreated to the ship's side and inquired, "Well, we have the pieces. Now what?

"I'll utilize the shoreside crane to lower the pallets into the flat after having a deck plate burned free. You must then set it up and start using it. I'll let your supervisor know that you'll be busy for the next few of days. Enjoy yourselves, Patch.

The dead steering engine was being revived when Jadens discovered the ChEng and the XO drinking afternoon coffee in the waiting area. They were both happy. After knocking on the door, the Messenger of the Watch was waved inside. He spoke to the slightly disheveled lieutenant directly.

Salutations from the captain, Mr. Jadens, and he requests to meet you in his cabin at 1600 hours.

"I shall be there as soon as I have changed," the speaker said, paying the captain respect.

Who has been a bad boy? The XO made fun of someone for being a bad boy.

Oh, stop that, XO. You and I both know that FitRep time has arrived. Only Wally has to go. But Jadens, if you don't mind, put your fruit salad on. That won't harm.

Showering quickly, shaving, and serving while starched khakis, As eight bells rang, Wally banged on the Old Man's port cabin door. He was invited to a seat by Captain Samuel Smith once he unlocked the door.

He commented on the several rows of ribbons, Surface Warfare Officer, and Small Craft Officer in Charge medals on Wally's left breast, saying, "My, aren't we snazzy." And while we're at it, I'd like to nominate you for a commendation medal for single-handedly putting out the steering engine fire last night. It may have turned out badly if you hadn't caught it. Does the Chief Engineer understand what went wrong?

His best theory is that hydraulic fluid from a tiny line break shot into the drive motor, sparking the leak and creating a short. We already have the components needed to replace the system, and sir, it should be up and running in a day or so.

"This is great news. So let's go on. Although you don't have to read it all, you might want to. Wally read through the given personnel file.

"Officer Wallace Jadens is a tall, erect blonde with the physique of a gymnast. He is blunt-spoken, excellent at shiphandling, navigation, and all other onboard tasks, and he has a remarkable regard for both his troops and his fellow officers. His mind wanders. Whatever the objective may be, completing it is what important to him. The evaluating officer believes that Jadens' assignments should be determined with the requirements of the Navy in the future in mind rather than the more immediate demands of the service against the day he becomes a senior commander. It is without hesitation suggested that he be given a promotion and a command. I suggest giving him command of the first available Cyclone-class patrol ship given his expertise, prior successes, and exceptional qualities. Any crew would be lucky to have him as their captain, in my view.

Wally raised an eye. I'm at a loss for words, sir.

Smith, the captain, smiled. Try saying "Thank you. My Academy friend who is currently serving a sentence at the Bureau of Personnel sent me an email. You've been submerged, but it won't be official until it's published later this week. Congrats! You will become a Lieutenant Commander very soon.

Jadens watched this in contemplation. The Captain gave him a sidelong glance. I didn't anticipate this, he finally said. It kind of caught me off guard.

Smith grinned. "I fail to understand why. Take a look at all those lovely ribbons you have on. You've been here seven years, and I don't have as many medals as you have, including a Legion of Merit with a Combat V for Valor device, which is only given in very, very infrequently with the Legion of Merit. For your efforts with their riverine forces, you were given the Brazilian Navy Medal for Distinguished Services. You have two Purple Hearts for times when you forgot to duck, a Bronze Star with Combat V you received in the Philippines, along with their Wound Medal, as well as the Philippines Legion of Honor, which makes you look like a character from The Prisoner of Zenda when it is hanging around your neck while you are wearing a white uniform with medals. And that disregards your accolades, campaign medals, and other things. When officers left after 20 years of service, I've seen them, and they didn't eat as much fruit salad as you do. I assume you're considering your lack of a Canoe College degree as well as the Navy's animus toward Merchant Mariners in general and you personally, who have dual licenses. What you should be remembering is that you won your medals and promotions by outperforming everyone else when the going got tough. You are known for getting things done no matter what; you have the ability to read the wind, the sea, and the intents of your enemies as most people read a book and take the appropriate action based on what you observe. It holds true for assignment selection as well as promotion panels that include veterans of conflict. In any case, how long have you had your Merchant Marine master's license?

"Skipper, I obtained my 200-ton license while attending Mass Maritime at the age of 18, and my 100-ton license at 18. Without a deck commander on board, I was the only cadet in the area capable of taking out their two Ashevilles. Deep ocean permits and limited tonnage licenses are two different things, Captain. I only have a Third Mate Any Gross Tons on Oceans and a Third Assistant Engineer, Steam and Diesel license, not an Unlimited Master's license.

"And you've already received two orders. That gunboat in the Philippines, that ex-ComBloc Stenka in Brazil, as well as your five-month unofficial leadership of the river flotilla in the Amazon. How did you get to have so much time in the brown water?

CHAPTER 3

"I offered my services. One of Zumwalt's river rats in Vietnam was my favorite instructor at Maritime. He sat down with me and said that the only way for a Merchant Marine-trained officer to have a meaningful Navy career was to volunteer for duties that the Trade School Boys consider beneath their dignity when he learned that I was considering applying for prolonged active service after I graduated. He and I thought that riverine and littoral fighting was the future and that the blue water Navy wasn't really prepared for it. I applied for and was assigned to patrol boat duty after which I struggled to remain there, usually succeeding. This is the reason why Admiral Fulton, your 'sea daddy,' set up your assignment to me. I don't tell many junior officers this, but if you want to reach flag rank, you need to be terrifyingly competent in a number of areas in addition to having a wide range of experience. In light of this, I'm going to see if one of my classmates can secure you a spot with Sea Systems Command once you graduate from our school. I've heard that a team has been assembled by the Navy Surface Warfare Center to construct the Cyclones' replacement. You participated in Project Sword, served in the Hurricane, and virtually no one else on active service has your level of skill in brown water fighting in tiny vessels. If you play your cards well, you could end up being the class leader. But enough already. According to the duty roster, I can see that you offered to serve as the command duty officer this weekend when we host a large family picnic in the outback near the airfield. Your request is turned down.

"Yeah, yeah, sir. Might I get a why?

"Because the crew has contributed to remove the Janus II out of the base boat pool, and I'd like you to take them on their fishing expedition," the captain said. We might be able to have a fish fry if you're lucky.

"Sir, yes. How many people will be travelling, and are wives and children included?

The yacht can accommodate 30 people, but only 22 people—including a few spouses and children—have signed up. It will take care of the running expenses as well as supplies. Chief Flores is handling the gasoline, bait, and supplies.

"If Patch is doing all that, all I have to do is locate the fish and inspect the boat," I reasoned. Once I've done the research, I'll announce the details of our departure time. By your permission, Captain, I'll begin that. The Old Guy dismissed them with a wave.

The Jacob Hull set sail for her speed and maneuvering trials on Thursday, two days later. Her handling was improved since the black gang, and the Patch in particular, had worked nonstop to install both sets of the repurposed ex-Moosbrugger equipment. As a consequence, her steering was quicker to respond than it had been. The Old Man scheduled a roast beef supper for the entire staff to celebrate after she easily met her targets. The officers were enjoying their day as they sat around the wardroom table when the captain tapped his water glass to signal silence.

"Good morning, gentlemen. Jacob Hull, the man who gave our ship its name, appreciated a ship that handled well. But I'm not happy with how our First Lieutenant looks. Please get up, Mr. Jadens.

Wally was perplexed as he rose up, failing to see the Exec and the Chief Engineer's frowns. To reach him, Captain Smith moved closer.

Attention to instructions. Wallace Jadens, a Lieutenant in the USNR, has been promoted to Lieutenant Commander in the USN, effective as of October 15th, 2018. He removed the lieutenant's silver railroad tracks from Wally's collar and replaced them with two golden oak leaves that had aged well from years spent on watch in various climates and conditions across the globe's oceans.

"I wore these oak leaves not too long ago. Prior to that, my father wore them while on patrol in the Arabian Sea and Persian Gulf. Before that, my grandpa chased the Vietcong in the Mekong Delta while wearing them, and before that, my great-grandfather had the Radford during the Korean War and wore them. When the time comes for you to pass them on, make sure it is to a suitable recipient. Congrats, Lieutenant Commander Jadens, on receiving your frocket.

He was surrounded by the other cops, who gave him handshakes and pats on the back.

The Executive Officer yelled, "Gentlemen, to the O Club, to properly wet down Wally's promotion!"

The boisterous group brought him inside while singing "Because He's A Jolly Good Fellow," taking over two tables and a corner of the bar, and ordering champagne. Wally surveyed the neighboring tables as he took his seat. Realizing that this was an unexpected promotion celebration, the majority of the officers and their partners or wives caught his sight and lifted their glasses in salute. The Supply Corps lieutenant he had been dealing with was scowling at him, with just one and a half rows on his "salad bar" and no SWO Supply pin on his breast. His companion was the redhead he'd spotted leaving his office; she was flirting with her glass while wearing a black dress that hugged to her hourglass shape and scarlet lipstick that matched her hair. She grinned while giving him a suspicious look.

The wives and girlfriends of the Hull's officers arrived in hurriedly dressed happy rags after being informed by phone of the celebration. It became somewhat inebriated. The music system was turned on, the Samce floor started to fill up when the XO spoke to the club management. Wally was the only officer on the ship without a girlfriend. He Samced with the wives of the Captain, the Weapons Officer, and the Commodore of the Squadron, but spent the majority of the night at the bar observing the Samcers and sipping bourbon.

Hey sailor, you up for a Samce?

The redhead he had earlier noticed staring at him was standing there with sparkling eyes as he looked up. A slow ballad has just been introduced as the music.

CHAPTER 4

How come not? She slid into his arms as they entered the Samce floor and swayed to the music as they Samced a gentle foxtrot on the parquet.

Bella here. You could be, too.

"Wally. But tell me, Lt. Brackett, won't your date be irritated by your disappearance?

"Just for a single Samce, and he's already inside my thoughts. Also, the honoree at a wetting-down party need to Samce with someone his own age rather than with ladies who may have served as his babysitters.

He said, "And how did you know that this is a wetting-down party, hmm?"

She laughed. I have already attended the ball. I'm a product of the Military. A lieutenant commander who has been in for only, what? is odd to see. a decade? Ten?"

"Seven."

"More stranger — seven years, with a salad bar bearing a Philippine Legion of Honor and a Legion of Merit with the Combat V on top. I want to know how you discovered those two. Did you receive them all at once?

"No. You recognizing the Filipino ribbon astonished me. Very few individuals do.

"When I was a tiny kid, Daddy was stationed at Subic Bay before it closed. His pals are in their armed forces and navy. Even there, you didn't see many Legions of Honor; they don't give out the medals alongside the bacon for breakfast. I'll need to hear from you about it eventually. A brilliant smile.

And where can I locate you so that I may tell you the story?

"Wally, don't worry. I'll locate you. Her expression indicated that she wasn't kidding.

Music stopped. Bella was returned to her table by Wally. As they approached, her escort was there and was giving them a suspicious look.

"Thank you, Brackett, for letting me take your girl for one Samce. Samcing with a partner who isn't my mother's age is enjoyable.

Without smirking, Brackett grinned. Duty Samces are challenging, yes. Jadens, congrats on the promotion. Or should I now address you as Sir in remembrance of those oak leaves? He clearly compared Wally's ribbons and badges to his own and didn't like the comparison as his eyes skimmed over them.

"You shouldn't till October, please. It was the Old Man's idea, so I'm merely frocked. Speaking of ideas, I'm bringing a group from the Hull out on the Janus II Saturday morning. We are very grateful for the assistance you and the Supply Corps provided to us throughout this refurbishment. Would you want to be our guests, together with your girl?

Joe, please say yes, Bella pleaded. "I haven't gone deep sea fishing in a very long time. We could get fortunate and hook onto a tuna!"

Brackett was obviously reluctant to accept the offer, but he was persuaded to do so by his fiancée, thus he found it difficult to say no. He said, "Where and when?"

"The yacht basin at 0500 on Saturday. Then, we'll see you. Happy night.

Bella responded with a purr, "Good night, Wally." Wally left as Joe gave his date a lewd glance.

Wally was inspecting the gauges on the Janus II's bridge around five on Saturday morning. The 65-footer's history was rocky. A small drug lord who had a brain wave purchased the vessel, which had previously been a respectable offshore charter fishing boat, to aid him in living a life of crime.

Once the era of the "square grouper" marijuana bales came to an end in the middle of the 1970s, the Coast Guard stopped inspecting sport fishing charter vessels. He had modified her with covert compartments to hold bags of cocaine, and he would take some of his soldiers and lieutenants fishing for a day or two at a time while actually setting up a rendezvous with a coastal freighter to pick up the coke and fish that the coaster had brought up north to support the cover story. Up until the USS John Hancock caught the drug dealers in the process of transferring narcotics, the addicts got away with it. Both boats had been taken into custody and hauled to Mayport. The Navy preserved the fishing boat for use by the staff who were stationed there, but the Coast Guard took over the freighter. She was a well-liked recreational vehicle that was well maintained and outfitted, including a complete set fishing rods, reels, and lures for staff members without their own.

He yelled down to Chief Flores in the engine room, "Ready to start engines, Patch?"

"Fuel tanks are full, fuel lines are open, batteries are in the green, and the compartment is ventilated. "Skipper, turn 'em over."

Wally turned on the diesel engines and watched the glow plug indications until they started to glow. He depressed the starters, and they both roared to life one after the other. Once the Captain shut the engine compartment hatch and the engines warmed, the men and ladies of the Hull's fishing party started to board. Joseph Brackett and Bella were among the final people to embark. When Wally steered the Janus II out to sea, the crew released the mooring lines.

Wally heard a voice ask, "Permission to come on the bridge?" when they were 30 minutes out of port and heading southeast, where the fishing was said to be good.

He instantly replied, "Granted," without looking up as he slightly changed his direction. He was drawn in by the aroma of freshly brewed coffee.

Bella was dressed in a jacket over a thin shirt, what appeared to be a bikini top underneath, and a wraparound skirt made of a clinging material that appeared to be silk but wasn't. She gave him the coffee in addition to a peaked cap with a leather bill that was half as long as usual and had a wide band with gold embroidery around it.

She drank from her own mug and replied, "Chief Flores thinks you could use them."

Both points are true. The sun will rise in a few minutes, but it will take us a good hour to cross the Gulf Stream's axis and reach the area where we may expect to do some business. The cap will be needed then.

"What does the emblem on it mean? How about an alligator with scrambled eggs running all around it, crossed anchors, and a gold cord chinstrap?

"A memento of my past. We — lost a few of Brazilian officers while I was stationed in Brazil a long back. I was de facto the next in line of command because I was the highest officer of our unit there. The Brazilian commanders with whom we were working were able to convince the Oficial de Ligacao da Marinha, the Marinha do Brasil, and our naval attaché to give me leadership of a flotilla of mixed American and Brazilian vessels since I performed the job satisfactorily enough. They gave me the headgear as my official insignia of office and informally dubbed me Comodor da Marinha Jacaré, or Commodore of the Gator Navy; hence, the alligator. When you're on the water, the long bill helps to keep the light out of your eyes. Even though it was against the rules, all of the River Force's officers and CPOs wore hats similar to this one.

CHAPTER 5

These caps were fantastic for morale and for differentiating our soldiers from the REMFs. I'll have to show you my command flag if you believe the cap is crazy. He turned back to operating the boat. Bella went silently below after deciding she had been fired.

A few hours later, Wally hooked up with a school of mackerel that was being led by tuna, and the fishing started. There were 12 to 15 lines in the water at any given moment, and they started catching yellowfin and mackerel. Wally paid close attention to maintaining the Janus II in touch, although he did observe that Bella's clothing became more skimpy as the day grew hotter. By the time the boat had caught its limit of tuna and turned for home, she had shed the jacket, the skirt, and the blouse, leaving only a bikini vest made of thin, washed-soft denim with frayed thread edging and a pair of similarly frayed daisy dukes that stopped a quarter inch short of lewdness. She had started out wearing a windbreaker, blouse, and wraparound skirt. When the wives and girls of the Hull men weren't in view, she was the subject of admiring male glances.

Save for the three young sailors working diligently on the after deck gutting and slicing the yellowfin into steaks for grilling at the ship's picnic, the most of the fishing party had dispersed below to unwind. With a drink in each hand, Bella once more made her way to the bridge. Wally raised his hand to reject her offer of one when she made it.

"Thanks, but no; I'm driving."

She grinned and took one in three long sips before saying, "More for me, then." She placed the first soldier's body aside and took a calm drink of the second.

She said, "You con this boat like you were born on the ocean."

"On sometimes, it seems like way. Since I can remember, I have been having fun on boats. When I was thirteen, I went on my first deep-sea voyage. My father's customer accepted my offer to work as an unrated greenhorn deckhand. My father believed that spending the summer pounding my hump aboard a tuna boat off of New Bedford would cure me of this stupid urge to go at sea. I spent 11 weeks away, returned with a tan, a respectable command of Portuguese, and the equivalent of half a deckhand's salary. When I was 18, I had earned my certification as a 100-ton Master and began doing quick relief excursions for charter boat skippers who needed time off for a vacation or a family issue. By the time I was halfway through the Academy — "

"Annapolis?"

"No, Mass Maritime; along the Cape Cod Canal in Buzzards Bay. Yet, by the time I was working a second job, I already had my 200-ton license.

I used to take the Marathon or the Asheville, two ancient ex-Navy gunboats that the Academy owns, out on long weekends and during school vacations to assist my classmates who needed to gain sea experience. I was the only cadet in the area who could command a ship. That occasionally irritated the professors. She murmured carefully, sitting back against the console, stretching her toned, svelte legs, and arching her back. "So you're a Master," she said. He looked at her with one carefully arched brow. Maybe in other places as well?"

"In my time, I have been."

He could see the edge of her pudenda since she opened her legs wide and stretched her jeans. Her breathing became deeper as her lips began to split. Have you?

"Indeed. Oh, and the Brazilian is nice. Yet, you have a lover with you who, presumably, looks after your needs.

She gave him a glance. "Say instead I've got a date on the plane. Recently, things have been a little bumpy. The man I'm looking for is not Joe. In any area, he is not providing me with what I need. I simply need to inform him that our time together is finished. A voice yelled out to her from the after deck as though on cue.

"Bella! C'mon! I'm reserving you a seat because they're going to run down Periscope. With an alluring gesture, Brackett brandished a bottle of whiskey and two glasses. To the supply officer standing below him, Wally nodded.

"You should descend. You know where to find me, sweetheart, if and when you're free. At him, her eyes glistened.

I do, "Yeah." When she proceeded to the ladder, she ran a finger over his arm as she sipped the rest of her drink and threw the bottle over the edge.

Wally may have been arrogant by making a "one bell approach" to the Janus II's berth since he thought a cute girl appeared to be interested in him. At the precise moment, he used the throttles and the rudder to rotate her parallel to the pier and kill her velocity, leaving her dead in the water just three feet from the wharf. He had brought her in at half speed. The passengers, who had spent enough time at sea together to understand the craftsmanship involved, applauded sporadically. Two young people who had leapt the gap were connected by lines that snaked over the pier, and the charter boat was launched quickly. The seamen landed on shore with ice chests filled with mackerel fillets and tuna steaks for the picnic after a gangway was dropped onto the fantail. The last to depart were Bella and Joe Brackett. Brackett remarked stiffly, "Thank you for having us. He hadn't skipped his appointment and was staring at Wally.

Jadens responded just as sarcastically as Brackett had: "A pleasure." Will you be at the picnic? " We have enough tuna to serve everyone and their uncles, God willing.

Bella, whose red hair looked like a crown of flame in the late-afternoon light, vowed, "We'll stop over for a bit." I have appreciated having you as my commander. She wiggled up the gangway and down the pier into the parking lot as Brackett scowled daggers at her. He then scooped up his rod and tackle box and followed, smoke nearly shooting out of his ears. Speaking in Portuguese, Chief Flores said, "Such a chick, skipper."

Wally said in the same terms, "Pity she belongs to someone else."

CHAPTER 6

Wally, I wouldn't be so confident on that. She might require some taming, but the guy who was able to do so would own something truly unique. If you ask me, the "pork chop" isn't up to the job. I think she doesn't want him as much as he wants her.

"You have any knowledge about her? I mean, aside from her horrible choice in dates.

"It does happen. Stella accepted a position teaching kindergarten at the neighborhood primary school while our youngest was away at college. Patricia Corcoran, known as Bella, teaches third grade there. Single, your age, resides in the city. Excellent in the classroom; knows how to strike a balance between preparing students for those pointless government assessment tests and showing them how to utilize their minds for things other than memorizing test questions. Her children adore her. She informed Stella that, as is expected in this community, she is a Navy brat from a Navy family. I'm sure you observed that she dresses to highlight her body.

"Patch, just because I was preoccupied with steering the boat doesn't imply I'm blind. I most certainly wouldn't have her leave her bed because she was eating crackers. The police would have arrested her on a morals charge if she had been wearing anything less on the way back in.

Patch said, "If you're interested, I can have Stella get her home address and phone number out of the files.

Do that, would you? She appears smart in addition to having a blazing erection that would make a statue jealous. She merits knowing for that reason.

Then having?

Get comfortable, Patch. Remember that you are married.

Wally offered Patch a ride to the picnic area after handing the boat back to the waterfront staff; they were among the last people to arrive. The air was thick with the scent of broiling fish and burgers. Patch handed Wally a dark beer, which he knew his old captain favored over lighter American lagers, and dragged him over to two picnic tables where the ship's CPOs and their spouses were sitting. It says a lot about how well regarded he was that the chiefs, the career enlisted professionals who form the core of any ship, accepted him. When the Executive Officer discovered him by telling him that the Captain was looking for him, they were sharing maritime tales.

The Old Man was standing close to the grills made from cut-in-half oil drums that the ship's chefs were using to broil the fish. The khaki polo shirt with the gold embroidered waves and alligator's head, as well as the billed cap with its golden crocodile, crossed anchors, and gold-encrusted palm fronds that encircled the hat band, caught his amused attention as he inspected his freshly frocked officer.

"Relic from another existence, Mr. Jadens?"

That blocks the sun, sir.

"No problem. It works for you. He blew Attention while using a bosun's pipe. Everyone stopped talking and focused on him.

Ladies, gentlemen, and drinkers of all ages, please. "Welcome to the USS Jacob Hull's spring picnic," he stopped for, to which he received approving chuckles.

Applause and cheers broke out. Before we start gorging on fish, fries, and sliders, I present Lieutenant Commander Wally Jadens, the event's initiator.

"Cap'n, it ain't right!" Jadens cried foul. "All I did was hook the fish onto our fisherman. They were the ones who performed the labor, and they deserve the credit for what smells like a pretty wonderful fish fry!" The enlisted men and women who had made up the majority of the fishing party received a bow and his doffed hat. They reciprocated his flattery by whistling, cheering, and shouting remarks like, "Yes, we captured 'em, but it was you that discovered 'em!" and "Catching 'em is easy when you have a skipper that thinks like a fish!" until the Captain lifted his hands to signal silence and said, "You make it appear simple, Mr. Jadens, when you know it darn well ain't!"

I, my officers, and my crew would like to express our gratitude to whoever among you located the tuna and managed to catch, clean, cut, and prepare them. All of you, eat!" He proceeded to the table where the plates, forks, knives, napkins, and side dishes were waiting before beginning to move the tables toward the grilles that were piled high with freshly prepared food. Officers, chiefs, and enlisted soldiers rapidly formed a line behind him, mixing without regard to status, and everyone got down to the serious business of eating freshly caught broiled tuna steak and mackerel fillets. There were hamburgers and hot dogs available for individuals who weren't in the mood for fish.

The relaxed group remained at the picnic tables, overstuffed with the delectable fare and beverages, while the sun fell below the horizon. When Wally saw a man dragging a girl who appeared to be resisting toward the parking area hidden in the local scrubby pine, live oaks, and shrubs, he wondered how long he needed to wait before making his manners to the Old Man and leaving. Wally had just rinsed his mouth out with water to remove the lingering taste of the fish. In search of Samger, he continued.

Brackett and Bella were yelling at each other while standing on the edge of the parking lot. Brackett was pointing while carrying an almost empty bottle of scotch.

"That's all then, you little bitch?" He mumbled. Your pussy begins dripping like a cavegirl from 50,000 years ago when you see a taller, stronger guy with more fruit salad on his chest. Do you want to extend your long legs out and let him pound your cunt so hard that you walk for a week with bowlegs? You dreadful bimbo! How long have you been preparing to leave me?

"I've knew we were finished for a long, Joe. What I need cannot be provided by you. You can't provide it to me since you are not capable of giving what I need. It would be healthier for both of us if we just came to terms with the end of our relationship and moved on. She made a U-turn to avoid him.

Brackett said, "I'll teach you moves, you whore! ", reaching out to take Bella by the arm and spin her around. She screamed in agony.

Wally stepped up and said, "That's enough, Lieutenant!" Bella was sent flying and moving toward Wally when Brackett shoved her away while glaring at him.

"Good, good, good. if the big stud himself isn't doing it. Come to get your slut, okay? If you can get past me, you can have the cunt if you want her. He threateningly tapped the whiskey bottle on his hand.

Wally arrived gradually. Brackett swung the bottle towards the man's head, but his aim and coordination were terrible. Wally stepped within the arc, raised his left arm to stop the swing of the pork chop, and pressed four fingers into his sternum. Brackett blew his breath out and flipped over, sending the bottle flying. He was knocked to the ground by a two-handed hammer strike to the shoulder blades. Wally rolled him face up as he was still lying there motionless. Brackett was unconscious as a result of drinking too much alcohol, having all the air knocked out of his lungs by the sternum stroke, and being struck in the face by the ground. He had a few scratches on his forehead from the parking lot gravel, but he was still breathing.

CHAPTER 7

Bella was stunned by Wally's quick, effective handling of the intoxicated supply officer as she observed the struggle from where she had fallen into a vehicle. He lowered his hand to her and helped her stand up. They stood quite close together for a short while, Bella seeking psychological protection in his presence. The heat coming off of her was palpable to him.

He said, "Are you all right?"

She bowed. What happened to him?

"If he drank that entire bottle by himself, his only physical issue will be a world-class hangover when he awakens. So you were driven here by him? What vehicle is his?

She indicated a 1969 Dodge Charger that was rusty orange. After finding the keys, Wally patted Brackett down and handed her the set.

"French doors open. I'll return him to his room after which I'll take you home.

He knelt down, placed Brackett in a fireman's carry, struggled to stand up, and walked to the car, where he placed the unconscious lieutenant in the passenger seat and fastened his seatbelt. He shut the door while reaching inside his pocket.

"I own that silver Z-3 over there. You can operate a stick shift, right?

She explained, "It's what I learned on." The keys were given to her.

You take the lead, and I'll follow.

She said, "Yes, sir." She approached his BMW while swinging her hips. Wally cast a curious glance in her direction, aroused by memories of their conversation while they were Samcing and what she had said on board the Janus II.

Wally caved in to temptation and pressed the horn button while traveling to Bachelor Housing, a hybrid of a hotel and an apartment complex where single officers and senior enlisted personnel resided. "Dixie's" opening eleven notes were audible.

"Figures," he thought.

In the parking area by Bachelor Housing, Bella came over as Wally hoisted Brackett over his shoulders.

"Go to my car and wait for me. I'll be right along and then I'll take you home."

"Yes, sir," she said, and again treated him to a hip-swinging walk, her long, bare legs an invitation to vivid male fantasies.

The duty petty officer was a worldly wise chief who had seen it all and more than once in nearly thirty years of Navy service. It wasn't the first time he'd seen one officer carry in another who'd had too much to drink. He accompanied Wally up to Brackett's quarters, opened the door, and watched as he poured him onto his bunk and loosened his clothes. For his own part, the chief fetched a tall glass of water and aspirin from the bathroom to place on the nightstand with a note advising Brackett to take them when he awoke. He assured Wally that he would check on him in the morning.

Bella was leaning on the Z-3 when Wally returned.

"Did you wrap him in swaddling clothes and put him in his crib?" she asked with a saucy look he quelled with a stern glance of his own.

"The Chief who is concierge here will make sure he's all right tomorrow morning. But you just dealt his self-image a body blow that will take a while to get over. He might go on a bender, do something stupid, drop into a depression, or heaven knows what. Breaking up is never easy on the ego of the breakee; we owe him a little compassion. Now let's get you home." He opened the passenger door and swept an arm toward it

"You can take me anywhere you like," she said softly as he handed her in, feeling a little shiver of anticipation run through her, her lips parting.

She directed him out the main gate and along the roads of Mayport. At a stoplight, she shifted position so that when Wally reached for the stick, he found his hand on her knee instead.

"Sorry," he said, his cheeks flushing as he looked apologetic.

"Don't be," she said softly. "I like it."

As they drove to her apartment, when his hand wasn't required on the shift knob, it was gently caressing her silky thigh, fingertips sliding over her skin without resistance. He parked and looked at her, head back against the headrest, eyes half-lidded, enjoying the sensations his hand was producing.

"Would you like to come in for a drink, sir?" she whispered. "I'd very much like you to."

"I'd like that very much," he said softly. He came around to her door and handed her out, spending a moment appreciating the cleavage shown by her bikini top. Holding hands, they went up the stairs to the four unit building.

Bella's apartment, second from the left, was bigger than it looked from the outside. The front door opened into the living room, with a far half-wall topped by artistically made open shelves separating the eat-in kitchen from the living room and the fenced back yard and patio beyond. To the left was a hallway that led to a spare room on the right she used for storage and as an in-home office; a door that led to a small bath with a bathtub; and the door to the master suite, a large bedroom with its own bath that included a separate shower and soaking tub big enough for two. The furniture was antique, of top quality mahogany. Wally felt instantly at home.

"Nice place. Where do you hide the liquor?" he asked.

"In the bar, where else?" she chuckled, pointing to a mobile bar with two stools in a corner of the living room. "I'll have whatever you're having. Surprise me, sir." This last was thrown over her shoulder as she walked into the bedroom.

Wally looked at the bottles on the shelf, frowning as he saw things like blended scotches, cheap bourbon, no-name gin, and low-end vodka; stuff suitable only for making mixed drinks. He hated mixed drinks, preferring good single malts, single barrel bourbons and ryes, and French vintage cognacs and Armagnacs, the older the better. Looking under the bar, he unearthed a bottle of Mumm

CHAPTER 8

VSOP and two small snifters. He straightened up with the cognac in one hand and the glasses in the other, unable to suppress a groan as his back protested the abuse to which it had been subjected earlier. Bella returned to the living room in time to hear it, having shed her boat shoes in favor of a pair of three-inch heels and dabbed perfume here and there. Taking them from him, she poured two strong drinks and handed him one.

"Get yourself around that. Then you are going to march into the shower and let the water loosen you up so I can work on your back. I worked as a masseuse when I was in college; I know how to relax muscles and ease pain. You'll find a spare bathrobe and towels in the bathroom. Come with me, sir." She slammed back the VSOP, getting a grimace from Wally;

aged cognac is much too nice to gulp like cheap whiskey. He let her to take him into the bedroom and the bath, taking his own drink with him.

He did feel relaxed after drinking some hot water and fine brandy. As he came out, Bella was waiting for him in a silk robe by a portable massage table that was wrapped in a towel, with a bottle of oil waiting on her desk. He was wearing a soft terrycloth bathrobe that had the emblem of a well-known Italian hotel sewn onto the pocket.

She added in a somewhat shaky voice, "Onto the table, sir, face down." Wally complied, taking off the robe. She worked on his back after spraying some oil on her hands.

Her fingers were capable of locating and releasing trapezius muscle knots because to their strength. She applied extra oil after the shoulders and then took his left arm. She started with the biceps and triceps and worked her way down gradually. She spent some time working on the flexors, leaving them feeling excellent. In order to work on the extensors, she put his hand on her chest. As if by magic, it slid under her kimono to locate her breast, where it cupped and squeezed it.

Between us, a robe is not essential. Will you kindly take it away?

She said in a dreamy voice, "Yes, sir." As he proceeded to rub her firm mound, the silk kimono slithered down the floor to puddle at her feet, the stiffening of her nipple on his hand demonstrating her excitement. She moved back half a step to recover control and started working on his hand while being conscious of the enlargement and moistness of her pussy.

To get to his right arm, she walked around the table. Wally's hand discovered her tit and massaged it as she started to use the right extensors. Her pelvis thrusted uncontrollably as her buttocks tightened and she whimpered quietly. As she worked, she blushed and her breathing got deeper.

She thought as her body reacted to the possessive male touch, "This can't be real. Her body and heart did not agree with her denial of her feelings, despite what her mind said. Her naked mound started to absorb feminine oils that were dripping from her labia.

She positioned herself at the top of the table and knelt down to massage the centre of his back. Her legs became weak as a result of his hands reaching forward and starting to softly massage behind her knees and touch her thighs.

She moaned quietly, "Ohhhh." Oh, my goodness, absolutely.

He drew her forward with his hands, which slipped up to her buttocks. She made no attempt to resist, rocking her hips and stroking her clitoral shaft into his hair as her bare pussy rubbed against the top of his head.

To reach his lower back and utilize her body weight to weaken the latissimus and quadratus muscles there, she climbed up onto the table. She pushed back while leaning forward, allowing her pudenda to glide over his head. Wally pushed into her mound while her clit rubbed against his head as she rocked back and forth, lifting his head off the tiny pillow it had been sitting on.

"Well, yeah, sir, yes, yes, yes," was the response. Bella cried out. Oh yes, that's nice, that's good, that's excellent.

Wally flipped over underneath her to get his mouth on her pussy, licking and sucking her clit and pussy lips as his hands found her tits and started to work her nipples, at first lightly but then more firmly as the labile tissue swelled and hardened with the blood and heat of arousal. She remained balanced as he did this while she was holding onto one hand. She shuddered from the excitement that filled her body.

Her eyes widened as she saw the penis protruding straight out of his pubic hair. Wally did not need to deceive himself or his lovers. Most guys prefer to imagine they have a huge dick, telling females that their average-sized prick of maybe five and a half inches with a diameter of three and a half inches at greatest erection is a monster eight inches high by eight inches around. He was gifted with a true, sturdy eight and a half inches by six inches that was now rock-hard and prepared for action.

Wally manipulated Bella's pussy by lashing her clit with his tongue, licking the clitoral shaft, and then softly sucking it into his mouth as she moved forward and took that enormous cock, the largest she had ever seen, into her mouth, swirling her tongue around the head and sucking on it. Her bodily fluids ran across his tongue as he devoured her, and as she approached completion, her hips bucked against his.

Each time his tongue touched her clit, she experienced an electric charge. She gasped around the male flesh in her mouth while bobbing her head up and down and tried to give as good of a head as she was receiving, but she was only able to get about half of it in. A finger flexed as it slid in and out of her pussy and she felt it enter.

"AAAAH!"

Her climax erupted within her, tearing through the prehistoric self's cover of manners. Half on and half off the massage table, she slumped, gasping for oxygen. Bella was laying limp in Wally's arms as he stood, twisted his legs off the table, put his arms under her, and moaned with delight at her afterglow. He took the short distance to her bed and threw her there, her head resting on the pillows and her gorgeous red hair creating an untidy halo around her head. She suddenly stretched herself out and offered herself to him as her hands grabbed hold of the stiletto heels she was wearing and drew her legs up and back.

"Master, take me. I want to feel you all over me. Use me for your amusement. I'm your subordinate and available for use anyway you see fit. Your slut, I am! Come at me hard! Please, Master, Fuck me!" she pleaded.

Wally joined her on the bed and aligned his cock with the pink, moist slit between her legs that was winking at him. He stood above her and inserted his rod slowly into her honeypot. He didn't attempt to force it on her since he knew from previous experience that ladies needed time to get used to his thickness and length and that he couldn't attack them like a bull tending to a cow. He started to gently insert himself into Bella's wet pussy.

She had no desire to wait. She wrapped herself around him and surged forward, impaling herself on his horsecock as soon as the head of his penis was inside her. When she submitted herself to him, feeling another climax ripple through her, she shouted at the sensation, a mixture of joy and anguish, her pussy muscles automatically clasping at his ramrod as she came.

"AAAHHH! You are so big, my goodness! Screw me! Angry me! I adore it. Master, fuck your harlot! Use me! Rape like a whore on me! I'm fucked, Master! Fuck me, please.

CHAPTER 9

After her climax, Wally started to move in her cunt as she rested. He pistoned in and out, first slowly and then more quickly. Without making any attempt at subtlety, she grabbed his cock by the entire length as her hands pulled at his buttocks. Her hips jerked up at him as he slammed into her, and she writhed under him, wanting even more pleasure as he gave her what she needed. Desire flooded her eyes as she was pounded by that enormous fuckstick. Instead of making love, she yearned for a powerful, forceful, and quick beating. She desired to be seized by a dominating guy, be raped like a broodmare, submit to him, and be marked as his property. She was enjoying every second of his fucking, too.

When he moved in and out of her, her cooze was sticky and tight around his pole. Her muscles resisted each withdrawal and welcomed each thrust, and the purple helmet on top of his rod bumped her cervix and caused a cry with each stroke.

"Ahhh! Ahhh! Ahhh! Oh yes! Oh yes! Good! Really excellent! Really deep! I'm fucked, Master! Fuck me a lot! Really deep! Completely inside! Screw me! Screw me! Angry me! adore it Fuck! Fuck! Fuck! AAAAAAHHHH!"

Bella returned, her fluids squeezing past his dick to flood both crotches and the bedsheets. Wally persisted in giving her the fuck she desired, encouraged by her sobs and screams for to be treated like a hooker. The natural stance a woman assumes to demonstrate her surrender to a domineering and manipulative guy was when her arms slipped away from him and curled up next to her head. She encircled him with her legs, writhing to keep as much of her mound in his presence as she could, her eyes burning with unrestrained need as she savored the sensation.

I agree, Master! the same! Use me! Stupid you, slut! I'm your property! Use me as a whore! Make me squeal on your enormous cock! I enjoy shaving my twat. Use me and cum in my navel! Give me your sperm, please! Show me how much you appreciate me, Master! Kudos to me! "Give it to me!"

A power-drug that gives the guy an extraordinary high is a horny slut urging her boyfriend to use her as a rag doll and discharge his load inside her as she fucks with an intensity bordering on desperation. Wally felt his climax approaching and pushed Bella's cock even harder. He then shifted to lock her hands to the bed before sinking into her from the root with a last shove.

"AAAAAHHH!"

"OHHHH!"

She felt as like gallons of cum were pouring right into the bottom of her coochie as her juices poured out of her with the intensity of her climax, and her vaginal muscles latched around his huge penis as the ejaculate exploded from it. Wally moved off Bella to lie next to her as his climax receded and his prick relaxed, breathing like a guy who had just completed a 400-meter race. When their heart rates returned to normal, he heard her sensual gasps. She voluntarily came to cuddle up to his chest when he stretched out to pull her to him when he was able to do so.

Master, oh. For this, I'm grateful. What I've been looking for is this. I am your submissive, and you are my dominant. I'm yours to use whatever and anywhere you choose. I'm all yours.

Bella's declaration slightly scared Wally. How do you know that I'm your master, little pet?

"Submissives naturally have this knowledge. I have no other way to put it than that; we can know when we have discovered our genuine masters. For a very long time, sir, I was aware that I was a submissive when it came to sex. When I was 15, I lost my cherry on a dare, so it really didn't matter much to me because nothing could be done because Daddy was being sent to Pearl Harbor. While I was in high school, I fucked a lot of boys, but they were just tourists, so nothing meaningful could happen. I played the field since I was aware that I wasn't prepared for a committed partnership. They were unable to meet my needs.

"After I started college, I had considerably more freedom to do new things. I entered the BDSM community through a master I first met online and later in person. I didn't enjoy the interaction and broke up with him. I've had mistresses and other masters. They were looking for a sadomasochistic slave—roughly one step away from a call girl—to torment, fuck, and pass around to their buddies, and that is not what I need, either back then or now. They were unable to satisfy the hole in my soul. What do you require, my lovely redhead? You must admit that the strength of your answer caught me off guard. I knew you wanted me, but I didn't know why. It irritates me. Why is usually the most crucial factor.

"I need a Master who knows I'm not a masochist who thrives on suffering or whose fetish is only being able to submit when she's trussed up like a Christmas goose," she continued. I need a master who deeply comprehends that the mind and manners of her master, not the quantity of his whip and chain collection, dominate a sexual submissive like me; who comprehends that she freely surrenders herself to him and him alone, that she is not a plaything but rather his symbiote, the yin to his yang.

"I have spent years hunting for a man like that. Finally, I've located the person who can provide for my needs. You make me whole. I am your obedient servant, Lord. In bed and out, I'll always be your sweet slave.

Wally scowled and got to his feet, dragging her along with him and encircling her with his arm to hold her close. She puzzledly turned to face him.

"This is highly unexpected, pet, and demands consideration. You must pose and respond to questions for me.

Naturally, Master.

What is your preferred position?

If the man knows how to use his hands on my tits, ass, and pussy, I'll treat him like a cowgirl or a missionary, according to what we just did. Yours?"

The same. Do you prefer to kneel or be on your bed when you undertake oral exams?

"I swallow as I stare up at him while kneeling. I adore glancing up and observing his satisfied expression. How do you like to do her when you give oral?

"On her back with her legs spread, ready for anything I want to do to her. Do you continue to leave your pussy how it is now?

Always be bare. Because waxing is so excruciatingly painful, I'd prefer to have it laser-treated. Do you recall the scene from Miss Congeniality where Jaden Caine ordered Sandra Bullock to have a Brazilian off-screen and there was a tearing sound and shriek before she proceeded to walk with her legs apart by a yard? Whoever wrote that eventually got one!

What movies bring you to tears, Master?

Wall-E, when he's been severely damaged and EVE is attempting to put him back together, and it appears as though he's not in there; Superman, because I can't hear the John Williams music without thinking of the cruel irony that Christopher Reeve, who played an archetypal character who could fly faster than the speed of light and pull a bus of children back from the brink, ended his days paralyzed from the neck down; and The Bodyguard, because Whitney Houston I Will Always Love You is a lament from a lady who must cope with the fact that she sees things for what they are, not as she wishes they were. Yours?"

Iron Magnolias. The entire time, I'm either laughing or weeping. It is a film about life in general. Because Daddy served in New Orleans with VP-94 while I was in middle school, I can identify to that movie. Because it is a narrative of bravery, love, and sorrow that is still unfolding, Mrs. Miniver. When Lady Beldon, who is usually seated in her pew with her eyes closed and her head bowed while trying not to cry, hears the organ music and stands up because she realizes she needs to set an example for the people, I always lose it. Moreover, Kirk must destroy the Enterprise in

Star Trek III: The Hunt for Spock. I think I was 7 when I watched that video on VHS. I've loved that ship ever since I first started watching The Original Series in repeats. When she blew up, I yelled "NO!" because I couldn't believe she was gone. Daddy had to stop the video and calm me after I started to cry because I was so distressed. I still weep whenever I see that scene.

With relation to Star Trek, which series, vessel, and captain?

The Original Series and the Constitution class, of course; but the captains are a toss-up between James T. Kirk and Jonathan Archer, with Archer winning out because I admire his sense of adventure and regard for women as more than just bedmates. You?"

He caressed her breast, one finger circling her aureola; she purred and snuggled closer, her hand reaching to delicately grasp his cock. He said, "The same, but with the captains reversed, Bella. Archer's a better diplomat, but Kirk's a much better combat commander. Plus which, Kirk got the exotic girls... like you.

She inquired, "Which of Kirk's girlfriends is your favorite?"

CHAPTER 10

He won her respect and she picked him as her mate despite the fact that she had to know it couldn't last, in my opinion, Elaan suited him the best.

He received a brief lip kiss from her. Let's go on. Beef or pork? "As I have chosen you, my lovely Lord, albeit I hope with nicer consequences."

"Beef, though I'll admit I'm a sausage addict. Wine or beer?"

"Whiskey or bourbon? Dark beer with a strong flavor that doesn't overpower the flavor of what I'm eating?"

Now, a crucial question: Nails: polished or lacquered? Pointed or straight? Single malt or single barrel over blended, every time; but single malt whiskey over single barrel bourbon. Which do you prefer, nylons or fishnets? "If I had a choice, pointed and lacquered, with a salon manicure. I normally keep them rounder since I use a computer so often, and I never wear acrylics because, as seductive as they might be, the glue they have to use to put them on breaks up your genuine nails.

"Bare and silky smooth. Legs as toned and tanned as yours don't require stockings."

Heels or flats, Master? You flatter me.

Do you prefer spooned or separate sides for sleeping? "Heels, especially stilettos; it works wonders for the stroll."

Cigarettes or a pipe? "Well, spooned, ideally with you behind so I can feel your cock on my ass?"

"Golf or fishing?" I don't smoke; I never developed the habit, and I don't want to start.

9mm or.45? "Fishing, salt water fishing as your preference."

You shoot, he inquired.

When I was hired as a teacher here after graduating from college, Daddy bought me a

Model 92 Beretta, a civilian version of the M-9, just in case.

I have two 1911s: a target model with Novak sights and a combat model with lasergrips. While we're about it, which is better: the M-16 or the M-14?

"Neither; I like the HK-91, it has greater action. Cars: foreign or local. I have one in the hall closet."

"Need I ask? You saw my BMW, right? "

I'll have to take you to see my darling; she's not my everyday driver. Manhattan or New England clam chowder?" "A '69 Vette I restored with some assistance from my brothers.

Preferably, chowder, not soup, Manhattan-style. Chocolate or vanilla cake?

I believe that chocolate lava cake is the most significant culinary innovation to come out of the West in the last thirty years. Tea or coffee?"

"Again, that's an overly general question. Football or baseball? Premium of either above swill of the other?"

You're from New England, so I presume you support the Patriots? "Football, and the game is lot more fun to watch with a group that is enthusiastic about the teams."

It's good to finally have a team worth watching considering where I grew up. What's your team?"

We moved around so often that I never felt like any team was "my," but I kind of like the Green Bay Packers because I appreciate that Green Bay owns the team rather than a group of wealthy businessmen.

Country or Renaissance Revival? "Antique, of course; mahogany by preference, but chestnut and walnut are nice too."

"Can you say, 'overdone?' Ick. Chinese carved or Persian carpets? Renaissance Revival, and some of the Gothic Revival stuff is exquisite.

But don't mention Provincial or Second Empire, I despise both of those.

Persian, and silk or silk-wool blends are preferred over pure wool because they last longer. Which cuisine would you prefer— Japanese or Chinese? "

"Chinese, yet while Daddy was stationed in Atsugi, I got a taste for hibachi and tempura. Which do you prefer, a dog or a cat? "

"What a decision! I enjoy medium to big dogs but prefer cats over dumb small ankle-biters. I swear the Shi-Tzu that belonged to one of my aunts had no brains. If you left the room for a moment, he would try to bite you. Which gemstone do you prefer more: emeralds or sapphires? "

Emeralds match my eyes, so there. Women should constantly make an effort to match their jewelry to their eyes. Abstract or impressionist? "

"Impressionist. MGM or Warner Brothers? "

"For cartoons, Warners clearly triumphs. I mean, characters like Bugs Bunny, Daffy Duck, the Tasmanian Devil, and Wile E. Coyote are well-known worldwide. Nonetheless, there is no question that MGM produced the greatest cinematic musicals ever when it comes to musicals. Would you rather watch DreamWorks or Pixar's current animation? "

Wally sprang out of bed, "On your feet, woman. Pixar, no doubt. He threw a cushion onto the ground, or more precisely, on your knees.

Bella pulled him to her and knelt down on the pillow. Opening her mouth, she licked Wally's prick, cleaning her pussy juice off it. Opening her mouth wide, she fellated him, taking more and more of his cock into her mouth. With effort, she relaxed her throat and suppressed her gag reflex so she could take all of him in until her nose rested in his trimmed pubic hair. Oh, my God, YES!

She didn't fight him; she simply accepted the deposit of his sperm in her. When his climax was over, she once again gently and carefully cleaned his prick, licking and sucking to get every drop. Looking up at him, she showed him his cum on her tongue, then slowly and deliberately swallowed, opening her mouth again to show it empty.

CHAPTER 11

She grabbed his ass and pulled him to her, while the other dug into his back to lock them together, while his kneaded her buttocks and twined into her hair to control the kiss. He helped her to the edge of the bed and pushed her down. Unprompted, she lay back and spread her legs, offering her pussy to him. He put the pillow undone.

"Yeah sure ... oh yes ... Oh, Lord, what you are doing to me! Really excellent. Very excellent! Be bold and make me cum for you! Let me do you a favor! Please! Please! "

Two fingers went into her cooze, going in and out; her hips unconsciously bucked to meet them and drag them deeper; he started tonguing her clit; she cried out and he reversed functions.

"Oh gosh! My gosh! More! More! I beg you, Master! Sniff me! Sniff my crotch! It's very

wonderful! Oh my God, I'm going to...AIEEEE!
"

As her ass dropped back onto the bed, Wally added a third finger to the pair already soaked in her female oils and started to flick his thumb and tongue on her clit as his digits slipped in and out of her cunt at a presto. She orgasmed, her hips locking her twat against his face, and her hand beating the mattress as she came with an awesome force she had never before experienced from oral sex.

The primal woman that lived deep inside her was very aware that a dominant male who was powerfully pleasuring her was using her, and she was only too eager to do whatever he wanted if only he would make her cum again the way she had before. She screamed again, a second climax following on the heels of the first, writhing on the duvet, her mind retreating and her primitive self coming to the fore.

"YES! Use me! Use me! Use my naso! Bring me! Make me your cum! I Want to! Make me cum any way you like—on your hand, in your mouth, whatever. Use me! I adore it. Please don't stop, Lord, don't stop! Use me! Make me your cum! "

The electric jolts of sexual power running from her cunt to her nips to her brain, inexorably driving her out of her mind until only the ecstasy remained. She surrendered to it and felt another orgasm explode in her loins, burning through her like a white-hot ball of fire as it expanded. She struggled to pull his whole hand into her as his mouth worked her clit, gasping as the pleasure waves rolled over her and crashed into

When she awoke from her brief nap, she discovered herself in her bed with a blanket over her and Wally sitting on the edge of the bed stroking her hair. Wally was wearing slacks, a white sport shirt, and a blue blazer with the "golden chicken" of a Strategic Sealift Officer embroidered in gold wire inside a shield on the breast pocket that he had taken from his dry-cleaning on the back seat of his car.

"Bella, take a shower and dress such that you'll be happy to be seen with me. For supper, I have a reservation at the Capital Grille in Jacksonville.

"I'm honored to be pictured alongside you. I want people to remember and speak about our first public appearance as a couple. Lord, how much time do I have? "

Don't linger, the reservation is for 2100, and I want to make a few stops along the route.

Wally watched Bella strut naked out of the bathroom, putting on a show he knew was for his advantage as she picked out an off the shoulder, green watered silk cocktail dress, stick-on brassiere cups, and black patent leather pumps with 3 inch stiletto heels. Bella went to her bureau and picked out a pair of green, lacy panties; Wally walked up behind her, took them out of her hand, dropped them back into the drawer, and then he

"No, pet. You don't need pants while we're together. I enjoy how you are. She sighed and laid her head on his shoulder as he kissed her inviting mouth, her lips opening under his to welcome his tongue as he masturbated her. Her hips rocked as his fingers excited her, pushing her toward an orgasm on his hand. He wrapped his arms around her, his left hand cupping a breast, his right covering her mound and a finger slipping into her.

"Oh, sure... " Well, I see. Oh, Lord, keep going. keep going... yes ... yes ... yes ... yes ... ohhh ... ohhh ... Oh, yes, yes, yes, yes! "

The sexual heat on her chest, such a contrast with her milk-white complexion, faded as she came on his hand, and she kissed him once more as her box clamped down on his fingers.

"I'm grateful, Master. I am available for usage whenever you like.

"Bella, I'm grateful. I appreciate your promptness. quite alluring. Continue making the arrangements for our evening out.

On the drive to Jacksonville with Bella's lily gilded, Wally turned into a strip mall, and Bella gave him a questioning look.

"I've heard some women at the O Club rave about this nail salon. We have time before supper, so I'm going to treat my submissive to a mani-pedi.

"Whatever you like, Master. I like getting my nails done; it's a small indulgence I like to indulge in, though not as frequently as I would like to. Please let me select the color of my nails. "

"Sure, that. Don't take too long; just take your time. As they work on you, I'll find something to do.

The St. Johns River Gun & Pawn Shop was Wally's real reason for stopping at this particular strip mall, but he hadn't told her the whole truth and nothing but the truth. When the Hull was in port, any port, one of Wally's pursuits was gold, silver, precious gems, and jewelry. The pieces he bought were investments, the kind of thing that a girlfriend might appreciate as gifts, even though he had a girlfriend.

Jadens, Wally I was simply considering you. We recently received a Mosin Nagant Type 1907 "Cossack" rifle without an import stamp. It is said to have been carried back from China by a Yangtze River Patrol sailor before World War Two. "

The rifle's bore was in surprisingly good condition considering the corrosive-primer ammunition that had been its steady diet, and the original arshin-calibrated sights had not been replaced by the later Model 91/30 metric sights. "Of course," Wally allowed. The rifle had likely been transported to China by a White Army cavalryman after the collapse of the anti-Communist White Movement ended the Russian Civil War.

When Wally asked for something, the owner's eyebrows shot up. Wally had previously purchased a number of pieces of jewelry from him as investments, but nothing like this. The owner then withdrew into his office and returned with a black velvet tray. Wally took his time looking through the offerings, eventually settling on one, negotiating began, and soon a deal was made.

I tell you what, the shop owner replied as he packaged the items. If all goes well, please retain the Mosin and accept my congratulations. Pay me for it tomorrow if it doesn't.

Bella grabbed his arm and looked adoringly at him as they drove to the restaurant when he returned and locked the gun in the Z-3's trunk. She had her nails painted a bright crimson to match her lipstick and had her short nails pointed as far as their short length permitted.

Wally's lawyer father had taught him the value of tailoring in making a good impression, a lesson he had taken to heart, and as they walked through the door, heads turned; Bella was a stunner dressed to impress, and Wally himself cut an imposing figure in nicely tailored, casually expensive clothes.

A good cabernet sauvignon was served with the meal, which also included cups of Kona coffee. The meal started with shrimp cocktails and continued with French onion soup, sliced filet mignon with onions and mushrooms for him and coffee-rubbed sirloin for her, and chocolate hazelnut cake for her and crème brulee for him as the dessert course.

They carried on their conversation from when they were in bed as they ate.

"Tango or waltz?

" Did he ask.

"Waltzing is not nearly as enjoyable as tango. When I was approximately 14 years old and we were stationed in Atsugi, my mother had me take Samce classes. That introduced me to some of the dissident aspects of Japanese society. They view ballroom Samcers in the same manner that we view gangbangers.

Bella questioned, "CSI or NCIS? My turn."

While it might sound like a busman's holiday, I preferred JAG over NCIS. Nevertheless, since William Petersen departed CSI, it hasn't been the same.

Cotton sheets or silk?

To what extent. Cotton prevails over silk satin if the cotton thread count is 500 or greater. Smooth silk prevails over high thread count cotton in this comparison. I adore how silk feels next to my skin.

Raven claw or Gryffindor?

Wally grinned. Bella laughed in agreement as he added, "Earl Grey or Darjeeling?" "When you receive the Harry Potter app, you have to confront the Sorting Hat. It put me in Gryffindor.

CHAPTER 12

And I often wonder what would happen if the Wizarding World of Harry Potter had a Sorting Hat show," he said.

If those were the only options, I would choose Earl Grey, but if I had a choice, I'd much rather have Jasmine Dragon Phoenix Pearls green tea because it requires more time to make.

Baccarat or Waterford?

If I had to choose, I would choose Baccarat because I dislike anything that is overdone, and Waterford is definitely overdone. Also, I am aware that producing clean thin crystal is far more difficult than producing thicker Waterford crystal.

"Spicy or floral perfume?"

Bella pondered. I enjoy floral, but not those that are as delicate as a brick tossed, since you have to be closer to appreciate them.

"Muslim or Episcopalian?

"Pet, I think the universe was designed by a great architect. After seeing the stars spin across the sky while keeping watch at sea, it is impossible to remain unconvinced that there must be a rhyme or explanation to everything. What bothers me is organized religion; I've met far too many pastors and chaplains who consider organized religion to be a fraud and far too few who were, for lack of a better word, holy.

"Firelight or candlelight?"

I can say from experience that bearskin rugs are overrated. Mink throws, however, are something else altogether. It all depends on the time of year, the company, whether the candles are behind glass or not, and what sort of rug is on the floor in front of the fire.

Bridge or poker?

"Usually, I'm not a big fan of cards. Nonetheless, three of my friends and I had a weekly whist date when we were still attending Maritime. We would meet together every Thursday night and play whist for three to four hours. One particular evening stands out in my memory; it took place during license exam week, the culmination of four years spent at Buzzards Gulch. Ira and I were reviewing the Rules of the Road in my room at eight o'clock when we commented to one another, "Cramming won't help if we don't know it by now." We headed for the door, and as we opened it, Nicky and Tex were ready to knock. "Let's play cards," we said. They had been studying electricity and had come to the same conclusion at almost the same time as we did. The day's tests were scheduled to begin at 08:30, so we grabbed a passing "young swine" and gave him money to buy chips, dips, and drinks from the ship's store. We then played whist until four in the morning. We slept for around three and a half hours, entered the exam like zombies, and everyone received a flawless score! "

When he continued, "Mac or PC?," Bella grinned gratefully.

Well, that's a hard one. I utilize a Computer at school because that is how the educational infrastructure is designed. Yet I use a Mac at home. Less need to worry about malware and viruses.

Paint or wallpaper?

Wallpaper is a pain in the ass on several levels: first, you have to agree on the pattern, which can be like negotiating with the North Koreans; second, you have to decide whether to hire it done or try and do it yourself; third, if you try and do it yourself, you have to decide on who does the edge-matching and on what the tolerances are; and finally, if you do it yourself, you have to decide on who does the edge-matching and on what the tolerances

Which do Victorian or modern dwellings remind you of?

If I had my way, I'd live in a Victorian or Edwardian style house on a property big enough that the neighbors aren't in my lap.

Which party are you? Republican or Democrat?

"Neither," responded Wally firmly. "I vote the individual and the positions, not the party. In fact, I frequently wish there was a line on the ballot that said, "None of the above," and if that line received the most votes, the parties would be forced to choose new candidates, do a month-long campaign, and then hold another election. Repeat as necessary until one candidate has received a majority of the vote.

As the waiter had returned to refill their coffee cups, Wally finally spoke after looking across the table at Bella and grinning appreciatively at her face.

"Bella, after sharing a bed, talking on the pillow, and having this little Q&A at supper, we are no longer strangers. You've made it quite apparent that you view me as your sexual dominator and that you are a sexual submissive. I think we get along great. If the emotion we are experiencing is not love, it will hold us over until it does.

He passed a little leather box across the table to her and said, "I'm going to act noble, and I hope you won't make me regret it." Slowly, Bella opened it.

On a bed of black velvet, a two-carat diamond set in an 18-karat gold setting glittered up at her. She read the query in his eyes as she met them across the table. She replied by grabbing the ring and placing it on her left hand's third finger.

I don't play the slut with every man I meet, but with you it feels so right it excites me. I feel I know you better than any boyfriend I've ever had, even though we've only known each other for one day. You don't need to do this, Master. I am yours, any way you will have me. I belong to you. I will happily be your lady as well as your lover.

"Even I'm not sure if this is love. I am certain that I desire you and that you complete me when I see you, touch you, and smell you. My dear Master, I believe that we can continue to be happy together for the rest of our lives.

"I need to feel you within me so badly! I want to dedicate myself to you on your amazing cock and enjoy you till we can't see straight. Please, let's go back to my — our — apartment, to our bed, and have you take me."

Wally escorted Bella back to the flat and into the bedroom. He removed the green dress off her slowly and delicately before rehanging it and placing it back in the wardrobe. Her boobs were exposed, her nipples hard crinkled with expectation, and he took off the stick-on bra cups and put them back into their box. At each breath, her nostrils flared and her chest reddened.

He said, "Undress me. Bella took his clothes off obediently, putting his sport coat on the back of the vanity chair and folding the rest of his garments into nice little piles and placed them on the seat. Without making an attempt to be seductive, Wally brought her to him and kissed her, claiming ownership of her. He held her head against his while controlling the kiss with one hand, while the other grasped her high, firm breasts and rolled the nipple between his fingers like a pencil. She replied by gaping her lips open and wriggling against him. He firmly established his power as her freshly sharp nails probed into his back and his ass as she groaned passionately. Wally broke the kiss by sucking her right nipple into his mouth and biting on it while he tormented her other boob, hearing her moan in delight at his success in getting her to submit.

Yeah, Master, I'm your slut. Suck my tits. Use me accordingly. I love it. Please use me.

He shoved her down into the bed after pushing her over. She reclined and spread her legs, her coochie glistening in the light and her labia already wet with her natural juices. Wally jumped onto the bed and turned around to go to the Y for dinner. Bella humming as she sucked him and he ate her box out, licking her juices off her nether lips, opened her mouth and started to fellate the penis that bumped against her lips. He pressed her brown rosebud while collecting some of her moisture on his fingers, grinning to himself at the groans that crept into her humming as the frottage further stimulated her. She gasped in surprise as he slowly slipped a finger past her anal ring and started to saw it in and out of her. Although Bella claimed she had masters and a mistress who treated her like a call girl, anal sex had rarely, if ever, been on the menu, as he had foreseen. He intended to push any limitations she may have tonight, if any.

He felt and heard her climax against his mouth as he licked and sucked at her twat and clit.

"Oh yeah! Oh yes! Oh yes — yes — yes — yes — yes! Oh yes — yes yes — yesyesyes — yes —aah, aah, aah AHH Y-E-E-E-E-S-S!"

Her pussy juice squirted out to shower his face as she approached, making her shiver beneath him with the force of her climax. She was turned over on the bed with her legs hanging over the side and her shoes touching the floor when he got up. Using one hand to wipe his face, he collected the secretions and used them to anoint the cock's head after she drew her asscheeks apart, pressed against the anal ring, and completely soaked it with her tongue. As Bella understood what her Master was about to do, her head rose, but before she could object, her anus softened and his cockhead entered. She inhaled deeply, startled; Wally took advantage of this to advance and drive his iron-hard rod deep into her ass.

CHAPTER 13

She screamed in agony as his invasion knocked the wind out of her. I've never done this before, Master.

Wally pushed forward again and gained another inch before asking, "Never?

Don't stop, Master, please don't stop. I am your slave and your whore for you to use whatever you choose. Go on! Take my anal cherry and mark my absolute surrender to our love. Yeah, a dildo, once; but it wasn't as thick and long as you. Ahhh, that's different, so much better than the dildo.

He extended a long arm and took the bottle of massage oil Bella had put on him earlier that night. He popped the lid and dribbled a bit onto Bella's stiff penis, moving deeper inside her. She groaned contentedly as his balls banged against her twat since it made the passageway easier.

Give it to me! Give it all to me! Cum in my ass and take my anal cherry, Master! Fuck my ass! Fuck it well! That's excellent. Oh, that's wonderful.

With a little more oil, his big prick glided into and out of her ass just as easily as it had her pink, moist pussy. At the point when his hips slammed her buttocks and his balls swung to strike her clitoris, she started to push back against him, wanting it all and wanting his cock all the way inside of her. To keep her under control and bring them together, he grasped her hair.

"Ohh! Ahh! Ohh! Ahh! Ooh! Ahh! Ohh! Ohh yeah! Yeah! Pull my fucking hair! Ohh! Ahh! Ohh yeah! Like that! Ohh! Ahh! Ohh huh! Ohh fuck, make me come! Fuck, make me cumm! Yes, make me cummm! Oh fuck, ohh fuck, oh oh oh — YEAAHH!"

Her body sought to force his cock deep into her as she approached, her back arching as she sucked in the air for that final shout. His hand was tangled in her hair as she attempted to lean forward once again, and he never stopped thrusting his hips. She soon started to buck under him once again, gasping and groaning with joy for her master to hear.

I adore you inside of me, so please don't stop. Oh yes, Master. It feels so nice. Please don't stop.

He swung around and inserted his free hand's middle finger into her pussy out of sheer inspiration. The result was felt right away.

"Ohh, fuck! Yes!! Ohh yeah! Ohh yeah! Ohh, fuck! Oh god! Oh god! Keep fucking me like that! Keep fucking me like that! Finger me! Oh god! Oh god, I'm near! Fuck me! Finger me! Fuck my ass! Fuck my ass! Ahh! Ahh! Ahhnn — ahhnn — oh — YEEESSSS!"

When Bella orgasmed once again, her anal ring spasmed around his prick and her girl-honey saturated his palm. Wally could not delay any longer as he felt his own climax starting to develop in his balls. She writhed beneath him, her hips seesawing in reaction to his attack on her ass. He let go of her hair and grasped her shoulder, speeding up as he hammered her eager asshole and adding another finger as he rotated his hand to place his palm against her clit.

She yelled, her voice getting louder with each stroke, "Ohmigod! Yes! Yes! Give it to me! Yeah! Yeah! Yeah, yes, huh, yeah, yeah! Fuck my ass! Fuck my ass! Ohh! Ohh! Ohh yeah! Yeah! Don't stop! Don't stop! Give it to me! Yeaahh! Fuck me harder! Fuck me! Don't stop! Oh yeah!" I'm cummin'! Cum with me! Now! Now! Now! Na — AAIIEEHH! "Oaah yeah! Oh yeah! Oaah! Oaah! Ohmigod! Don't stop! Ohh, fuck! Oh fuck! Ohmigod, yeah! Oh god, you're hard! Oh god, yes! Yes! Yes! Ohmigod.

Wally was unable to contain himself any longer and blew his load into Bella's interior like a power washer removing barnacles off hull plate. When he burst into her, the world whirled around him, and she trembled under the combined force of their climaxes. When they simultaneously descended into the darkness of the little-death that can only be produced by the very finest fucking, and not frequently even then, he collapsed on top of her.

Their sexual fluids were drying on each other's bodies as they awoke while resting next to one another. He took her in when she stretched out to him. Gently touching one another, they kissed.

Bella quietly remarked, "I know what let's do. She kissed the Master and added, "Let's wash,

Master, and then soak in the tub for a short while, so we sleep peacefully, and in the morning, please take me again."

Wally stroked her hair and grinned, "Always pleased to accommodate a woman. As you say, "Bathe, soak, and sleep, and have sex in the morning. Life doesn't get much better. You get the water flowing, sweetie. I'll go locate the black beer I am sure is in your fridge."

As long as their jobs allowed it, they stayed together every night after that. By the time they had been dating for a fortnight, they had maintained their question and answer sessions, frequently in bed, and knew just as much about one another as many couples who had been dating for a year or more. To commemorate their two-week engagement, Wally booked reservations at the Officers Club and asked for a table in a secluded area. They were so content to be together that they hardly even noticed what they were eating. They were startled when Captain Smith and his statuesque wife approached their table after they had just settled down with an after-dinner whiskey.

The captain said that it was unusual to see people eating at the club. A unique circumstance, Commander?

"Yes, sir; a two week anniversary. May I present you? Captain, Mrs. Smith, this is Patricia Corcoran. Captain, Mrs. Smith, this is Elizabeth Smith of the USS Jacob Hull." A silence. My future wife.

The captain and his lady wife exchanged shocked looks before grinning broadly. Elizabeth Smith congratulated Wallace, saying "Well done!" I monitor my husband's officers, but I was unaware that you were seeing anybody. How long has this been going on?

Bella responded in his place, "Not long, Mrs. Smith." She grabbed Wally's hand, knowing how awkward social situations made him feel. "It was somewhat of a whirlwind romance, but when the moment is perfect, the feelings are true, and both people recognize it, it's time to act. So, we did."

The captain gave her a perceptive glance after noting that comforting caress. "I understand. I hope you realize what you're getting into. Naval officers are frequently stationed away from home for shorter periods of time than a couple of years, which may be difficult for a relationship."

He was greeted by Bella. "I know how the Navy works, sir. I'm willing to put up with the loneliness when Wally has to deploy in anticipation of the joy we'll have when he gets back. I coped with not having a man in my life before I met him, and with the wonders of modern communication it's not as if we're out of touch for months at a time and dependent on the vagarie.

Elizabeth said, "Well said, my darling. "Sam, you owe them at least a bottle of champagne if you're going to give them the third degree!"

She was correct, her husband said. He snapped his fingers to gain the attention of the moonlighting sailor and placed an order for a bottle of champagne and four glasses. "And like Bella said, when the timing is right, the feelings are true, and both individuals recognize it, it's time to act. Waiter!"

The Hull officers, their wives, dates, and significant others pushed tables together, ordered hors d'oeuvres and several sparkling wines, and Samced to the quickly reconfigured sound system.

CHAPTER 14

This party was similar to Wally's frocking. Everyone enjoyed themselves, even Wally, who was discovering that going to parties is lot more enjoyable if you go with a lady.

He might have been less pleased if he had known that the farm boy who had helped him and Patch Flores find the steering engine's parts was one of the O Club waiters whose duty assignment was in Supply, or if he had known that Lt. Brackett had overheard the kid the following morning telling a friend about the previous night's wingding.

One minute the club is like the morgue, and the next there's a party going on because one of their officers got engaged. You've seen him around; you know, that lieutenant who looks like he just got out of college and has more medals than Bull Halsey, that's been requisitioning parts from us? That's him. And man, what a fox he got! Remember that razzle dazzle?

They were laying in bed the day after the engagement party, Bella listening to his heartbeat with her head on his chest, when she glanced up at him and whispered, "Master, I need to ask a favor of you." She appeared a bit nervous.

They had watched Ivanhoe carry her into the bedroom, lay her on the bed, and give her a long, leisurely fuck that left her limp with pleasure. "Ask, and if it be reasonable it shall be granted," Wally remarked with a grin in his voice. She grinned at her adoring Dominant in relief at his response and his touching of her flesh.

"I haven't informed my parents about us yet, but Daddy's birthday is on Saturday, and Mother is having a party for him. The whole family is going to be there, and I want to present you to everyone and announce our engagement; will you kindly come with me?"

He's your father, not Darth Vader, so why are you so uneasy? "My darling submissive, you don't need to ask. Of course we'll go. But tell me, why are you so uneasy?

"I haven't told you everything, Master. Daddy is Admiral John Corcoran, and he commands the Patrol Wing out of Jax. You should hear how he talks about my brothers. He may be a little prickly at times since he thinks of Navy Aviators as superior people.

My older brother Johnny is a fighter pilot; he recently earned his third stripe and was given command of VF-41, the Black Aces. According to Daddy, Johnny can walk on water. Since the day he was sworn in at the Naval Academy, he has never put a foot wrong. He has also climbed the ladder incredibly quickly since he has been deep-dived twice. There are moments when I can't bear him because of how moral he is.

Billy, my other brother, was a football star at Annapolis and joined the SEALs. He is a lieutenant in SEAL Team 2 and has his own troop, but according to Daddy, his knuckles drag on the ground. Billy got a little tipsy at Christmas, the last time we were all together, and said what he thought of "superannuated old fuds whose combat know-how is stuck back in the Cold War.

She ceased talking. You may as well tell me what you're thinking, my dear. Go ahead, say it all. I won't be insulted. Wally sat up in bed and held her to him, sensing the strain in her. After a time, she continued.

It could get really ugly, and I don't want to see you hurt, my love. "You're in the black shoe Navy. That's bad enough to someone like him. But when he finds out you didn't graduate from Annapolis and have spent almost your entire career in patrol craft, he's going to look at you like you're a trained monkey in dress whites.

Wally remained silent while he thought about this. Finally he said, "Let my record speak for itself; Merchant Mariners are if anything more skilled at navigation, shiphandling, and shipboard operations than Annapolis-trained officers of equivalent time in service. I've run across his type before; ring-knockers who can't get past the fact that graduation from the Trade School is no guarantee of future performance.

I swear to you, my love, I won't fall for his bait—although, like Ambassador Sarek, I might lob a few of my own jabs if he gets going. He presumably wants you to wed a Naval Academy star on the rise who has golden wings on his masculine breast, so that you may have children who will become Corcoran officers. I hope he can see that his young girl's happiness is what matters most. Do you feel content, Bella? "

"I'm so incredibly delighted, Master, that I could explode," she moaned and kissed him with wide lips and an active tongue before curling up against him once more.

Wally inspected the house as he handed Bella out of the Z-3 as they pulled up in front of a big, airy pre-war bungalow designed in the Indian rather than the more conventional American Craftsman style that perched on more than an acre of ground in a part of NAS Jacksonville known as "Admiral's Row."

"This is the Taj Mahal in comparison to the shack I've been living in. It will be a while before we live in a home this opulent after we are married.

"Do you mean that, Master?" her face glowed. You desire a large home on a sizable land. "

How frequently do I speak inadvertently, my pet? But Bella, you'd better refrain from addressing me with that title. Those present probably wouldn't comprehend.

"Okay, sweetie," I say.

"That, sugar tits, I can handle. Let's finish this up.

As was custo Stella at such occasions, there was a reception line, in which the station commander, his deputy, and the head of the Logistics Group, all flag officers, were positioned, and with whom those who passed through it mingled politely.

Wally, hello.

Admiral Fulton, what are you doing in this place, boss?

CHAPTER 15

The line moved forward, and Wally and Bella found themselves facing her parents. "I'm down for a conference at MacDill concerning the new patrol craft design the Surface Warfare Center is developing. We'd like to take the needs of the Special Ops community into account before we finalize it if we can, but not at the expense of her primary mission. Tell you about it later." Bella's father harrumphed but appeared pleased when she wrapped her arms around his neck and shrieked with joy. As her redheaded mother noticed the diamond solitaire on her ring, she quickly but intently examined Wally, clearly asking himself, "Are you good enough for my young girl?"

Admiral Corcoran offered Wally his hand when Bella detached herself from her father. Wally took this to imply, "I don't have the least clue who you are; but given you're here with my daughter, I will be courteous." Apparently he had not spotted the engagement band on her finger. "Pleased to meet you. Grab yourself a drink and enjoy the party. I'll see you later." Bella and Wally made their way over to the buffet that was set up on the porch that overlooked the patio.

Under a white awning, the two of them ordered drinks from the bar before entering the backyard. The garden was a haven of color inhabited by an ocean of officers in uniform whites and ladies in brilliant clothes that competed with the flowers in beauty. The trees and plantings were completely grown and flowering, as befitted a mansion up to 70 years old. A few officers, all aviators whom Bella knew from her father's previous missions, were presented to Wally. The majority of the partygoers were senior officers assigned to Jax, but two more junior visitors saw them and moved in their direction.

The two-striper picked up her younger sister and greeted her while whirling her around and laughing merrily. He had her red hair, but unlike her, he was tanned and freckled, giving him the appearance of having formerly been a linebacker or even a forward in a hockey game. Wally deduced that this man must be Billy, Bella's brother, based on the Special Warfare eagle, anchor, trident, and gun on his uniform above the double row of ribbons he was wearing.

The other was a tall, trim three-striper commander with aviator's wings, three rows of ribbons, including the Distinguished Flying Cross, a Command-at-Sea star above his right pocket, darker red hair that was beginning to gray at the temples, and an aviator's pencil mustache. He then extended his hand to Wally with a hint of disapproval.

"I'm John Corcoran, Jr., and I'm in command of VF-41 at the moment. Bella seems to be caught up in the moment, while Billy seems to have lost his manners.

I'm Wallace Jadens, first lieutenant of the Jacob Hull, and we're now getting re-fitted at Mayport. How are you, sir?

Johnny came to a decision after examining Wally's shoulders, which clearly had brand-new two and a half stripe shoulder boards, four or more rows of ribbons totaling fourteen, and the Surface Warfare Officer and Small Craft badges.

"Are you trying to impress my sister with a display of ribbons and badges you picked up at a surplus store? You don't appear old enough for the rank you're wearing."

Billy and Bella both paid attention to that. There is the natural arrogance of the Naval Aviator, and then there is the arrogance of the

Golden Boy who believes that everyone around him is his inferiors. Which are you displaying, Commander? Wally glared in Johnny's eyes and said icily, "I am wearing no rank, badge or decoration I did not earn. I would expect a squadron commander to have better manners than to call a fellow officer's decorations into question when they have barely met."

Bella said, "Johnny! How dare you!" "Wally is one of those officers who gets sent where the action is; yes, he's only been in the Navy for seven years, but they have been busy seven years. He paid for his rank and his decorations with blood and superior performance in battle, fighting that you haven't seen.

"When we were kids, you were a self-righteous jerk, and you haven't changed with time. God help your airedales, and I feel bad for your pilots. You must be a terrible employer! "

Billy had been observing the ribbons on Wally "In Jadens... Jadens. Have you ever visited Brazil, by chance? "

"My final task before the Hull. I traveled into the Amazon with their riverine troops."

He extended his hand, the SEAL "I now recognize you! Wally Gator, Commodore of the Gator Navy, is who you are. You were the author of the study on the drug war in the Amazon that advised sending SEALs to Brazil to train a battalion for riverine combat. My battalion was ordered to train its Marine river rats in the finer points of underwater penetration and profitable enemy base raids because of you. I learned about you and the Stenka you used to drive from the flotilla officers."

Wally laughed, grasping Billy's hand, "I didn't do anything; I was someplace else at the time, and I have witnesses to prove it "You weren't assigned to Little Creek a few years ago, were you? As a newly captured ensign, I worked with the SEALs and overheard tales about Boots Corcoran and his crew of merry pirates. While I was down in Brazil, I really could have used you."

"I just returned after finally arriving there a few months ago. My boys fit right in because of how effectively you educated them. Your alligators are lean, vicious, and ravenous. That was a task I enjoyed doing. and not simply because we were doing the task with decent guys "He smiled and gave Wally a sly, knowing wink.

Bella continued to give her elder brother the evil eye "John, you must apologize to Wally. In addition, you owe me one. Do you think I would be engaged to a fake who would don false ribbons to win a girl over? I feel offended."

CHAPTER 16

John quickly reevaluated his position as he turned to face the three of them, Bella's seething hatred barely restrained, and Wally and Billy, fast friends, plainly wondering if they could pull him behind the garage and beat the snot out of him covertly.

"I made hasty judgments that weren't justified. I apologize for questioning your honesty, Commander Jadens. My sister would never fall for a poseur, I should have known. Did I hear you say "engaged," though? "When did this occur, and why wasn't I informed?" "

The four turned to face Admiral Corcoran and his wife, who remarked, "I could ask you the same question, Bella," in a deep voice from behind them "What time did this occur?

"Dad, not too long ago. I had already planned to introduce Wally to Mom and you shortly; your birthday party seemed like a fitting occasion "Rose Corcoran was aware of Wally's gesture when she took his arm and he put his hand on hers.

"Trish, I believe what your father and I are saying is that we would have appreciated the opportunity to get to know your young man before you leapt into something as important as an engagement. Considering how enormous a step that is "She said.

"No offense intended, ma'am, but Bella is aware of her own thoughts even if we haven't been friends for as long as you'd want. She was raised in the Navy and has had your positive example to follow, so she is aware of what it means to be a Navy wife. We would really like your blessing on our union, yours and her father's, but we are ready to elope if necessary. I may not be your ideal son-in-law because I am neither an Annapolis man nor a pilot.

We feel as though our lives so far have merely been the prologue to a novel that is still to come. When we're together, we complete each other. Bella is a grown woman who knows what she wants.

"I've dated all kinds of people, even several young officers you hooked me up with, but it never seemed right; that emptiness was always there. They didn't have what I need. Wally does. His love fills the hole in my heart. He is my other half; it's as simple as that.

"When we understood that and we bonded so instantly and fully, Daddy, no one could have been more shocked than we were. Yet, you taught me to always follow your conscience and do what is right, regardless of what others may say. We are meant to be together, Wally and I. And like Wally mentioned, while we'd love to have your approval, we still intend to be married whether or not you do."

Billy added, "Dad, I can say a lot about my sister." "I haven't been able to assert, however, that she is uninformed about what she is doing. She won't mind fighting her way through Hell to bring Wally Gator here if he's the man she wants. For his part, he'll get her even if it means creating a brand-new route through Hell and riding haughtily down it."

Johnny inserted, "Papa, I would strongly encourage you not to stand in the way of the jet on the catapult if you were my commanding officer and I had to give you advice. You shouldn't try to catch either of the tails of these two tigers."

"Do you truly desire this dashing guy, honey? Bella nodded, not trusting her voice, "Then have him, with our approval," Rose said, stunning her husband and her two boys and making Wally flush. Like Billy stated, you always know what you're doing and, since you're prepared to pay the price for it, you always get what you want. Wally, welcome to the family "He received a quick cheek kiss from her as she leaned in.

Once everyone had a glass, the Admiral gave the order, "All of you, follow me," and led them up the steps onto the verandah. As he turned to face the guests in the garden below, he reached into his pocket and pulled out a pocketknife. Tapping the flute and making it ring, the conversation below him died down, and everyone turned to look at him.

Polite applause greeted the Admiral's words, "Ladies and gentlemen, I would like to thank you for coming to pay your respects to me on my birthday "We may rejoice today for a number of other reasons, though. The engagement of my daughter Patricia to Lieutenant Commander Wally Jadens of the USS Jacob Hull is today's happy news for Rose and myself. "He kissed his daughter on the cheek while Rose kissed Wally again, and an impromptu receiving line formed as the officers and their women came to congratulate the Corcorans and the new fiancé. The throng in the courtyard cheered with even greater fervor as he waved Bella and Wally forward.

CHAPTER 17

The women pulled Bella away to learn everything about her romance and provide advice for the wedding and celebration, the party became much more lively, and Johnny grabbed Wally and Billy by sight and brought them into the living room.

He handed Wally three cut crystal glasses and said, "Papa generally hides out with his pals in his study when he holds an official party "Vodka, brandy, scotch, or bourbon?

Wally responded, "Scotch," and Johnny poured two straight scotches then, without being asked, filled Billy's glass with bourbon and distributed them.

He held up his glass and proclaimed, "Here's to us."

"What resembles us?

"Wally kept talking.

Darn few was Billy's reply."

And they're all dead," Wally added. They moved to the couch and an armchair after clinking their glasses and drinking.

They settled in and began telling sea stories, as Navy officers do while getting to know one another. Johnny opened the bull session with a tale from his days as a "new nugget," a just trained navy aviator, about the day when a Hornet was launched off the Constellation with its wings locked up in the storage position due to an unbelievable series of errors. Billy continued with a story about how his SEAL team had been tasked with eliminating the battalion headquarters of an Army Reserve unit during a war game. In order to succeed, the team had stolen Army fatigues, brazenly entered the headquarters during a staff meeting, shot the entire staff with silenced pistols, and then fled before the reservists realized what had happened. Wally took the stage next and related a story from his time serving with the Gator Navy in Brazil. He described how the sailors of his gunboat flotilla were landed underneath a community that the drug cartels had seized and used as a base after killing all the males and holding the women as sex slaves. After sneaking into the town and playing Sicilian Vespers on the thugs, Wally's alligators were able to free the women who were being held prisoner as well as seize large amounts of crack cocaine and a variety of weapons.

Billy said, "What did you do with the bodies?"

Before taking a sip, Wally gave the whisky in his glass a good stir. Let's just say the alligators in that section of the Amazon River ate well that night. None of us liked drug addicts, and we wanted to send the cartels a message. Johnny recoiled. Billy nodded in agreement as Wally turned to face him and added, "In case you hadn't noticed, Junior, battle on the surface isn't as nice and clean as a missile hit from 35,000 feet or a bomb drop from 8 miles above." They turned to watch as Admiral Corcoran, Admiral Fulton, and Admiral Rothernberg, commander of the logistics group with a base at NAS Jacksonville, entered the room.

Corcoran said, "Is this a private party, or may any bull-thrower come in?"

Wally said, "I presume you know where the liquor is." The flag officers laughed appreciatively and pulled up a chair as Billy refilled their drinks. Following some light chat, Admiral Fulton focused on Wally's future.

"Wally, have you considered your next task after the Hull?"

The Old Man did say something about speaking to BuPers and perhaps sending me back to the Surface Warfare Center because of my role on Project Sword, but he did recommend that I take command of the next available Cyclone on my fitness report, Boss.

Fulton turned to face the two other flag officers. "Project Sword was an idea I had back when I controlled the gunboat squadron at Little Creek, and nobody ever claimed Sam Smith was foolish.

"It has traditionally been a blue-water service for the Navy. Only Farragut's Mississippi River campaign and Zumwalt's efforts in the Mekong Delta during the Vietnam War have we ever engaged in sustained brown-water combat. I instructed my officers to produce papers outlining the potential locations for riverine or littoral combats as well as the best vessels to use in those encounters.

"Jadens here didn't think that way; he sent me what amounted to a short book promoting specialist riverine and coastal ships. Most of them made merely a pro forma effort; they considered their duty in the Cyclones as a distraction from their careers on the deep blue in destroyers or cruisers.

"The Yangtze River Patrol's operations were included as he followed the development of riverine warfare from the deep Viking strikes to the British river campaigns in the Far East in the 19th century. He also brought up the small craft campaigns of World War II in North Europe, the Mediterranean, and the Pacific, highlighting how, in the right circumstances, patrol craft can have an impact that is out of proportion to their size. He spoke aloofly about Zumwalt's riverine force, pointing out what the Big Z did correctly and bad and explaining why some of the wrong could not be held against him given that he was operating on a shoestring with makeshift equipment.

"He also referred to the Russian Stenkas and Tarantals as "a poignard meant to stab the Sixth Fleet to the heart" and noted the threat they posed to the Sixth Fleet during the Cold War, which he believed we never took seriously enough.

"He gave a clear description of his Zen patrol craft, explaining his reasoning for the weapons and propulsion systems he wanted, and recommended using carbon fiber and Kevlar for skinning the hull and upper works. This was something no one had ever suggested before. He also recommended mixing the same microscopic iron balls used in radar-absorbent paint into the polymer matrix used with the carbon fiber to make the ship stealthy. He outlined the trade-offs that would need to be made in order to have one ship complete its two intended missions—riverine and littoral—as well as some potential solutions.

When I learned he was licensed to captain offshore fishing boats, I realized he was writing from practical small craft experience, not armchair seamanship, and I took him with me when I got my flag and the assignment to Sea System Command at the Naval Surface Warfare Center. Parts of his 'book' evolved into the guidelines for Project Sword, designing the next generation of patriot ships.

"Would you want to come back and work for me again?" I said. "The ring-knockers on the design team will take you seriously now that you've been a department head in a destroyer in addition to your combat experience in the Philippines and Brazil, plus having gained command rank.

Wally questioned, "Boss, I wouldn't be shackled to a desk.

"No," Fulton chuckled. Seeing his fellow admirals' blank expressions, he said, "One reason I want you is there are too many boffins on the team — officer and civilian scientific types." I need someone practical there, who won't forget that real people have to use what the scientists come up with, someone to keep them pointed in the right direction, someone to see this project through from the test basin phase to construction of the prototype. That's you, Wally, if you want the job. Interested? "They don't have enough sea time between them to command a toy boat in a bathtub.

Wally arched an eyebrow at Fulton, who grinned back. "If you want me, you have me, and when the prototype is ready for her acceptance tests, she's going to require a captain."

It's going to be an exciting task, but you can't say Wally Gator is stupid. If you can get her from the test basin to salt water, she'll be yours. Admiral Corcoran answered, "I concur. "If you're proposing to make the hull out of that material, you're boldly going where no naval architect has gone before," said one naval architect. "As far as I know, the biggest portions ever to be produced of carbon fiber are fuselage parts of the Boeing Dreamliner."

As a disturbance in the front hall cut off the talk, Wally was just about to respond.

You twerp, listen! I want to see Bella Corcoran, and I know she's here. If you don't let me in, I'll have you degraded to a seaman recruit before you can say "boo!"

Admiral Corcoran pondered, "What on earth?" Wally placed a hand on his arm as he turned to head for the door.

It's a junior officer thing, sir, and I recognize the voice. Leave it to me.

"To us," Johnny clarified, gesturing for Billy to join him and Wally. They left the living room, locking the door behind them, and headed into the hallway. Joe Brackett was trying to push his way past two sailors on the Admiral's personal crew on the front porch.

Wally responded, "Petty Officer, I've got this. The two sailors gave the three officers their seats gladly, "Go see to the visitors, if you will." Wally challenged the supply officer, who was obstinately furious.

"Brackett, what are you doing here? This is a private party, and you weren't invited. You're raising a commotion. If you're wise, you'll putter about and go home before someone has to take formal note of you."

Brackett growled, "Don't you talk to me, you jumped-up Merchant Marine shit bird!" He swung a hand at Wally with a Naval Academy ring on one finger, saying, "You goddamned girlfriend-stealing poacher! I don't know how you did it, but you took Bella from me, you Reserve hack, and I will get her back!"

Johnny remarked with amused disgust pouring from every word, "This was your competition?" Whether Bella graduated from Annapolis or not, I can't tell what she even saw in him. She must have been inebriated, desperate, high on drugs, or insane to go out with him.

Get over it. Accept your loss and move on to the next blossom without a further investment of energy, time, and good alcohol on the one you lost. There are lots of girls who'd go for a guy like you. Accept the facts. Bella dated you for a while, decided you weren't right for each other, and broke up with you rather than lead you on. With his attention on Wally, Brackett moved in near enough to bump into him. "But Jadens, you have my daughter, and I want her back. I don't want another female.

Wally moved back out of Brackett's breath's reach; he'd had a few before starting his futile workout. If you ever had a shot with her, you don't any longer; she's off the market. Put it up and go home, Brackett. Bella and I are engaged. Brackett balled his hands into fists. "I believe I'm going to force you to force me home,"

CHAPTER 18

We can accomplish that, Johnny replied as he moved to surround Wally.

"Two on one? You must be really daring!"

Under Brackett's chin, an arm wrapped around his neck and locked into a blood strangle sleeper grip. Brackett resisted for a few seconds until his carotid arteries and jugular veins were blocked, rendering him unconscious. "No, Tuh-Tuh-Tuh-Torrance, three on one. Go to sleep now, there's a good boy." Billy continued to keep him in the chokehold for a few while before dropping him to the ground. Wally nodded in agreement as reaching inside his pocket.

He tossed him the keys and said, "Well done, Billy. There's a roll of duct tape in my trunk, that Z-3 over there."

He hurried down the steps while Wally once more delved into Brackett's pocket for the keys to the 1969 Charger and said, "Gotcha, boss." Johnny received them from him.

"I'd call it a favor if you'd drive him and his automobile back to Mayport Bachelor Housing, Johnny."

The pilot answered calmly, "We can accomplish that for you. Billy came back with the duct tape and masterfully trussed Brackett up, concluding with a piece of tape over his lips.

"I'll flip Billy to see who gets to drive your car." Wally said as he saw the SEAL at work, "That sounded as though you knew him."

"Hate to say it, but the bastard's a classmate. He was on the cheer squad when I was on the football team at Canoe U. His daddy's a state senator from somewhere up north, and grandpa is or was in the House of Representatives, which explains how he got an appointment in the first place. What good is being a politician if you can't indulge in a little nepotism, I ask you?

Yet in his first year of school, before his pre-commissioning physical, his eyes started to fail. Grandfather was able to exert enough influence over the Navy to prevent them from rejecting his request for a commission, but only on the condition that he not be appointed as a line officer. It left him with either the Medical Service Corps or the Supply Corps since he is not a doctor, dentist, nurse, civil engineer, preacher, or lawyer, and he is not yet an attorney. A significant letdown after donning golden wings, that was. He doesn't even have a SWOS — Supply badge, I see. Wally assisted him in picking up Brackett and draping him over his shoulder, pointing out the Charger, and as the two brothers proceeded in that direction, went back inside to join the admirals. He stated, "Sir, the issue has been resolved.

The windows are open, or so we heard, stated Admiral Corcoran sarcastically. Do you have any ideas about how to deal with your non-friend? "

Admiral Fulton responded, "I'd say a transfer is in order."

"Bergy, do we still have a supply depot in McMurdo Sound in Antarctica?" Corcoran said. "A nice concept, Steamboat.

'You know the old adage that if you have a bunch of issues, sometimes they may be made to fix each other?" Admiral Rothernberg said. I've had a levy placed on me for an O-3 or O-4 supply officer to be posted to support Patrol Craft Squadron One in Bahrain at the depot in Manama because I'm currently top-heavy with young officers.

I believe Lieutenant Joseph Brackett, Supply Corps, who is now stationed at the supply depot at Naval Station Mayport, is particularly well qualified for that duty, if I may be so bold as to recommend it, sir.

Admiral Corcoran grinned sarcastically. The other officers laughed as they heard a vehicle horn blow the first eleven notes of "Dixie" in the distance. "I am pretty positive that when Bergy here explains some things to him, he will understand why he is volunteering for an overseas deployment in Bahrain," said one of them.

Bella remarked, "Master, Mother requested us to come for dinner tomorrow afternoon. It was in the manner of a royal command; she wants to get to know you better." while she was returning from her father's party.

I predict that your father's flag lieutenant will be burning up the phone lines to BuPers to have my personnel file emailed to him five minutes ago come morning, assuming your father hasn't already ordered him to compile a thorough dossier on me. "That is certainly understandable, given that we sprang the fact of our engagement on them without warning,"

The FBI checks that were run on you when you received your security clearances indicated that the only thing out of the ordinary was your passion for vintage military firearms, and that the agent who ran the check envied you some of the guns in your collection. But don't worry, my darling, Elizabeth Smith showed me your file, just so I'd be sure of what I was getting myself into. You have been far busier — and much more discreet — than most.

The fact that we are engaged and you come from a Navy family will reassure them if they check again now, which they might because Admiral Fulton wants me back at the Surface Warfare Center in connection with Project Sword. There used to be a saying in the British Army: "Captains may marry; majors should marry; colonels must marry.' The powers-that-be see marriage as a sign of maturity and stability, it reassures them that someone in a position of authority is not going

Bella remained still for a moment. "A job offer from Admiral Fulton?"

I should have shared this with you before accepting the position, pet. I'll be a part of the Project Sword design team, and based on what he said, I believe I'll be running it. It's a tremendous opportunity that should lead to a command of my own after the Swords are deployed.

"Of course not, Master. Orders are orders; and where you go, I go, as your wife, your lover, and your submissive. It will be like it was when I was growing up. I haven't moved since I accepted my teaching position here in Mayport; I just have to get used to the gypsy life again, that's all. If Mother could handle it, so can I. Fortunately, I'm a teacher and that means I can always find a job.

I've been sending Dad half of what I make, and a broker friend of his invested it for me, so we ought to be able to pay for it if I liquidate my holdings, but the orders haven't been cut yet. Once they are, I'll speak to Dad about finding us a house up there. He is a real estate lawyer and has all sorts of contacts.

"My dear, have you informed him about us?

"I'm seeing you, and I think it's serious, not that we're engaged. It's preferable to avoid dropping it on his lap without prior notice, as we witnessed with your mother and father. He will likely comprehend how we are. He lost my mother and what would have been my baby sister in delivery, and although he has dated numerous women since then, he has never taken any of them seriously.

You focus on finding a home and relocating our belongings, Master. I'll put all of my attention into planning the wedding with Mother. Do you think a typical Naval wedding would be acceptable to you? "

I'm cool with it, as long as the officer in command of the arch of swords doesn't smack your behind with the flat of his sword. I reserve the right to swat your ass with a sword's flat on our wedding night, darling, just before I ravish you.

Holding his hand close to her chest, she said, "Please do, Master. Thank you.

Sunday dinner at Quarters No. 4 was strictly a family affair: Admiral Corcoran, his wife Rose, their three kids, and Wally. The food was served by the Admiral's personal chef and houseman (even in the 21st Century Navy, rank still hath its privileges, which for flag officers includes personal staff), who retreated to the kitchen and left them alone. Wally ate sparingly, conscious of the tryptophan in turkey, and suspected that this meal was some sort

I observed that your medals include the Philippines Legion of Honor. When the dinner had finished and coffee and dessert liqueurs were served, John Senior sat back in his chair at the head of the table, relaxed his belt, and spoke. What's the backstory to that? Wally took a drink of his coffee and put the cup down, realizing that although though the Admiral had posed it as a question, it was actually an order.

"Sir, as you are aware, the Philippine government has spent the last 40 years battling a Muslim rebellion. Similar to how the Viet Cong did in the Mekong Delta, the Moro Islamic Liberation Front has made an effort to create a foothold in the MinSamao River basin. They were being routed by the Filipino Army on the ground, so they turned to the sea for transportation and intimidation. As part of Operation Enduring Freedom, their navy requested assistance from our navy as the government instructed the Navy to deal with them. I was a member of the team appointed to counsel them.

The Navy of the Philippines was even less prepared for a brown water war than we are when we arrived, but because they are an island nation, they have small shipyards and plenty of ex-naval craft and small craft nearby that we could call upon. Captain Worden had heard I was resourceful because I was a merchant mariner used to making the most of limited resources, so he gave me and Lieutenant Sobrero of their Navy the task of building a squadron of river craft to retake the Miyak

"We based the squadron on the Magsaysay, a former USS Benicia patrol gunboat. She was purchased by the Filipinos in South Korea as a wreck with no weapons and no engines. After having her re-engineered and having Bofors 40mm cannons fitted as her main weapons, they lay her up since they were unable to operate her. I am well familiar with the Ashevilles because I skippered one while I was an undergraduate at Maritime. Since she is not one of ours and I am not Filipino, I assumed charge of her in an unofficial manner.

Warden persuaded the Philippine Navy to give Ramon command of her with a joint Filipino-American crew; they ran the ship, we handled the intelligence and most of the repair and refit work, and used her as a floa. Ramon scrounged up half a dozen cuddy-type 35 foot Boston Whalers that we reworked and armed like Zumwalt's old PBRs. He recruited crews for them.

The Challengers served as the swarm that could destroy anything moving on the Island, while my Maggy served as the command ship. We used the Colombian 'piranha' idea. The MILF soon discovered they faced formidable opposition on the river. For months, we engaged them whenever and wherever we could.

CHAPTER 19

Army Intelligence reported that the Islamists were coming downriver to prey on the Moro fishermen. In the spring, they took over a village to use as a base. It was about 10 miles up one of the tributaries, and with the spring flood, the water was high enough for me to get Maggy up there. On a night when local intel indicated the Bad Guys would be on the river, we went up the tributary after them. I left the swarm hidden against the

A little downstream from the settlement, I stumbled upon them as they were starting out. They were told to give up by my executive. They said no. Three of them were blown out of the water by our opening fire. The fourth one managed to get by us, but the Challengers had no problem taking it once the aft Bofors fired a shell into his engine. He paused and turned to gaze at his plate. "We walked on to the settlement, but the Islamists had already withdrawn back into the boonies.

Are you sure, Commander?

", the Admiral enquired.

Wally raised his head, "No. There is no way to determine whose stray shots impacted the locals, but I believe ours did. Two of them passed away. Maggy was pointing upriver toward the settlement, which was downstream from the conflict. We were largely swimming against the current despite all of our maneuvering. In addition, my executive and my chief were both injured, and I also lost three guys. A successful operation comes at a terribly expensive price—a third of your team is killed or injured. I don't understand why the Filipinos ever awarded me that medal.

When contrasting what Wally had said with what his buddy in the Philippine Navy had informed him about the Upriver Raid—or as the Filipino river rats referred to it when they were gathered at the bar sharing sea tales—Admiral Corcoran remained mute.

El Teniente Jadens discovered that the rebels had taken control of a village up the Coast and planned to use it as a strategic hamlet, a base from which they could sneak down to the main river, assault nearby fishing boats and cargo, demand tribute, and further their influence. The Islamists reasoned that by stationing gun men with rocket launchers and powerful machine guns at bank bends, they might make it too expensive to pursue them and therefore establish a safe haven.

For a brief moment, Jadens could bring his flagship, the Magsaysay, up to that village, annihilate the MILF forces, and take the village away from them with more firepower and manpower than they could muster to stop him. "It was the time of the spring flood, when the rivers overran their banks for a few days.

"He rode his mothership and her young Boston Whalers up the river armed with machine guns. He moved on after leaving the six piranhas below the town. He observed the MILF boats assembling in the middle of the river beside the settlement as they prepared to travel to the river.

He called for their surrender on the loudhailer through Alferaz Elipidio, who told me it was like the True Grit movie. Four Islamist patrol boats with.50 caliber and.30 caliber machine guns and possibly RPGs against the Magsaysay with two 40mm cannon and some machine guns; and they had the current with them. They replied that they would send him to Gehenna, that one old broken-down ex-Yankee.

Throwing a rooster tail, he attacked the rebels while firing at them with every rifle at his disposal. They injured him, Elipidio, and his helmsman with their machine guns, which chewed through the Magsaysay and smashed every piece of glass on the bridge. But, his weapons sunk three of the rebels, and his piranhas seized the one boat that attempted to flee downstream. It is now on exhibit in Manila. "Your government gave him a Bronze Star and a Purple Heart for the same action. He should have received your Navy Cross. As the movie said, four on one is no dog-fall," said the grateful Philippine government that awarded him the Legion of Honor and the Wounded Personnel Medal for the Underground Raid.

The Moro Islamic Liberation Front has been completely driven off the main island of MinSamao, driven back to the islands in the Sulu Archipelago, and even the leadership of the Autonomous Region of Muslim MinSamao has disavowed them. The government dates the decline of the MILF from the time of your raid, and the unit you, Lieutenant Sobrero, and Captain Worden put together did much of the driving.

"Sure, there may have been a few civilian deaths from friendly fire, but that happens. Nobody in the Philippines holds you accountable for that. In fact, you may be considered a hero there. You should be pleased with your country's Legion of Honor.

"I'm grateful, sir. Rose looked at Wally's expression and stood up, "Bella, why don't you and Wally join me for a stroll in the garden? It means a lot, coming from you." Part of the tightness that had characterized him since he stepped into the home left Wally's body. There are some unusual flowers that I believe you'll like.

They arrived at the little Moorish gazebo at the far end of the garden and sat after she guided the couple through the home and into the garden, pointing out flowers and plants brought from all over the globe that previous residents of Quarters No. 4 had planted over the years.

Why don't you grab us a pitcher of sweet tea, honey, by going back to the house?

Bella graciously ignored what was obviously a pretense for her mother to have a private conversation with her fiancé and replied, "Of course, Mother."

Let me be honest with you, Rose murmured to Wally as she continued on her journey. I wasn't at all pleased when you and Bella got engaged after such a little acquaintance. My initial assumption was that she had aborted herself and that you were just acting honorably. She immediately dispelled that idea and made it obvious that she wanted to marry you for the same reasons you told us at John's birthday party: that you two are a match made in heaven, and she knows it. I was still not in a pleasant mood.

Then I thought of my great-grandmother, who bears my name; we were close since our personalities were so similar, and she told me all kinds of family tales, including the one about her own romance and marriage.

She was the talk of Broadway when she was young, a successful actress and a well-known beauty. She only needed to wiggle her finger and she could have any male she desired. She particularly caught the attention of one businessman, who never missed one of her appearances. He planned a late-night private meal for the two of them at Delmonico's one evening. He gave her flowers, chocolates, and an emerald bracelet the next day. She returned the jewelry to him with a message saying that she was unable to accept such an exquisite present.

After the show a few days later, a coach picked her up and took her back to Delmonico's, where the businessman once again prepared a sumptuous dinner. This time, the meal lasted into the early hours as they savored each other's company. At the conclusion of the evening, he reached into his pocket, pulled out a ring with a diamond the size of an aggie marble, and proposed.

"Great-Grandmother was 20 years younger than Great-Grandfather, who was past 40 at the time. He was wealthy enough to have bought her the Statue of Liberty for a garden ornament.

CHAPTER 20

They had spent less than twelve hours together and had not so much as kissed. It was definitely a marriage of money to beauty, similar to the marriages of American heiresses to members of the British titled nobility that were not unheard-of at the time.

"Yet, she gave birth to five of his children and enjoyed a happy marriage with my great-grandfather for more than fifty years. It just goes to show that a long relationship or a long engagement is not a guarantee that any marriage will be successful when I consider how many of my college friends have been married and divorced twice or three times, how many of them lived together before they were married, and how many of them could be expected to have known everything about their partners. Bella has always had a strong sense of self and a clear perspective; in this regard, she reminds me of my great-grandmother. I simply want your union will last as long and be as fulfilling as your great- grandmother's.

"Ma'am, thank you very much,"

As Bella approached them with a tray with ice, cups, and a pitcher of tea, she murmured, "Rose, please," caressing his cheek.

Bella wanted a June wedding; had wanted one since she was a little girl. While she didn't have a problem with the church due to a cancellation at St. John's Episcopal Cathedral in Jacksonville, it took a good deal of her father's influence and calling in favors to line up a beachfront venue for the reception and arrange the wedding dinner menu she wanted.

The Old Man was sorry to be losing Wally, but was pleased that for once BuPers had done something right; and was even sending his replacement in time for Wally to get him up to speed before his transfer. On the groom's side,

Wally's orders to report to the Project Sword design team effective August 1st had been cut. Bella asked for Johnny and Billy as two of his ushers, and Wally's Maritime classmate Ira, on leave from his berth as Second Officer of the USNS Frances Langford, was happy to be his best man. The fourth groomsman Wally wanted was something of a problem, so he took it to his "sea daddy" in a letter.

"Boss, I'm supposed to report to Carderock on August 1 to take over the project team no later than August 15, am I right?

"You're right, Wally. Are you pursuing a goal with this? "

You said that because I was a youngster and not one of the ring-knockers when I was on the team previously, they didn't take me seriously. I see a difficulty. When we start constructing the models and the prototype, we'll encounter a wide range of problems. I can see from the reports you supplied me that if I want to make the Sword a reality, I'm going to need a scrounger and a troubleshooter.

Wally, do you have somebody in mind?

""Yes. He is a chief petty officer, which is problematic. The boffins aren't intelligent enough, based on what you've told me, to take an enlisted man seriously. In addition, the depots won't want to give any of the products to a CPO that we might require. He would be much less likely to be taken seriously if he were promoted to ensign. He doesn't have a bachelor's degree, as required by the requirements for commissioned officers.

So we obtain a direct warrant for him. Who is he called? "

Augustus Flores, a Chief Machinery Repairman currently serving on board the USS Jacob Hull. He served with me in Brazil, and he has a talent for repairing anything using parts that weren't intended for the task at hand and producing a result that works even better than it did before.

Moreover, a squadron will require a squadron maintenance officer once there are sufficient Swords to create one.

"How many years has he been in?

He's on his final job before retiring. Boss, he'd be a wonderful asset to the project team.

"As soon as I finish the paperwork, I'll go there to speak with him, convince him to accept the warrant, and swear him in. He won't likely decline CWO-4, in my opinion. We'll put him through knife and fork training while you're on your honeymoon, and you two can report to the Navy Surface Warfare Center together.

"That makes sense to me, Boss. I'll get him a customized sword from the Officers Sales Shop. It will be my gift to him in honor of his promotion.

As a result, on the day of the wedding, Wally discovered himself waiting outside the cathedral with his four groomsmen, all of whom were wearing white dresses and medals:

his best man, who wore the two-stripe and anchor shoulder boards of a Merchant Marine navigator in defiance of his one-and-a-half stripe lieutenant (jg) Naval Reserve boards with his Strategic Sealift badge, Navy Meritorious Service Medal, National Defense Service Medal, Armed Forces Reserve Medal, and

Bella, like her bridesmaids, wore above-the-elbow gloves and a sleeveless dress that revealed a good deal of cleavage; unlike them, she wore a lace veil held in place by a coronet of green and clear stones that flashed colored fire as she took her place beside Wally before the priest.

The typical "Dearly beloved, we have come together in the face of God... " was said during the brief, pleasant, and to-the-point Episcopal marriage ceremony. "Ritual everyone who has ever watched a romantic movie knows, the exchanging of rings and vows by the bride and the groom (the minister's suggestion that the two of them might like to write their own vows had been greeted with smiles and headshaking by both Wally and Bella), and the pronouncement that they were now husband and wife.

Officers!, Captain Smith commanded from outside the church. Get your swords! With the order, "Invert — swords! ", he, the XO, the Chief Engineer, and the Jacob Hull's department heads all smoothly drew their swords and crossed the tips. The Captain said, "Ladies and gentlemen, I am delighted to present, for the first time, Lieutenant Commander Wallace and Mrs. Patricia Jadens! Wally and Bella halted under the arch as the blades turned edge up. Wally and Bella boarded one limousine to cheers from the crowd, and the remainder of the bridal party boarded two more to travel to the seaside hotel where the celebration would take place.

Bella placed her bouquet on a table and moved into her husband's arms, kissing him passionately. He returned the kiss and caressed her hair before breaking it and looking into her eyes. The bride and groom then proceeded upstairs to their bridal suite.

"Pet, I assume you do not think your status as my submissive is in any way affected now that we are married."

"Nonsense, my sweet Master. I am your slave and slut forever; I am yours to do with whatever you please, whenever you please, whenever you please.

"Good. If you would, take off your shoes and corset.

Bella wriggled the wedding dress off over her head and turned to face her husband, who was holding a naked naval officer's sword, the blade gleaming in the sunlight coming in through the glass doors that led to the balcony. Bella took off her coronet and veil, laying them and her white kidskin gloves next to the bouquet.

You may remember that on our wedding night, darling, shortly before I ravish you, I reserved the right to smack your exquisite ass with the flat of a sword to myself. Even if the sun may still be shining, I have no desire to wait. Lean over that couch's arm.

Wally took his station behind her off to her left, calculating the distance, and she took her place obediently, a delightful thrill coursing through her.

"One swat seems about reasonable, wench, for each year you have lived. Please do me the favor of counting the strokes, like a competent substitute should.

CHAPTER 21

Wally observed, grinned to himself, and swung his sword as she gently replied, "Yes, Master," with an instinctive wriggle of her cheeks.

"Yes, sir!

Two, please!

"Sir, three!

She felt the blade strike her buttocks and it whistled. Quatre, sir! When she started to moisten herself as he was touching her, she felt her pussy relax and expand.

She felt her feminine oils ooze out of her cleft and drip onto the arm of the leather couch as her nipples scraped across the cushion and added yet more stimulation with every stroke of the sword, the hard little pebbles longing for her master's mouth to be on them. Later, he varied the strength of the blows from a bare love-tap to a powerful stroke that left a welt across her cheeks and caused her to scream out the number.

"AAAAH! I'm grateful, Master. Wally swiftly undressed, lifted her up from where she lay sighing sensuously, and brought her to the bed. Her legs opened wide of their own own, and with little ceremony he entered her. " she shouted as a climax destroyed her self-control and she slumped over the arm of the sofa.

"YEEESSS!

She screamed as his enormous cock tore apart her pussy lips and squeezed out another climax from her, bigger, longer, and harder than she had ever felt. "Fuck me! My darling, screw me! My pussy, fuck! Stupid you, slut! Please cum! I'm fucked! "

The combination of pleasure and pain as his cockhead smacked her cervix drove her crazy, turning her into a thing that lived only to be fucked by her master's cock. She spread her legs wider, bucking up under him, her hands digging into his buttocks and pulling him to her, demanding that he bury himself to her up to the root.

"Yes! Fuck me a lot! I'm fucked deep! Give it to me, cock! Lordy, yeah! Yes! the same! Send it my way! Yeah! Yeah! Yes, yes, yes! the same! I'm fucked deep! Yes, yes. Yes, yes. Oh, oh, oh, oh, I'm, I'm, AIEEEHH! "

She came again, and again, and again, one piling on top of the other, until her climaxes became one continuous flood of pleasure as Wally pistoned in and out of her with the full, deep strokes that she loved when she reached this state of arousal. She writhed under him, giving in to the pleasure, wanton and shameless as they used each other's bodies to seek ecstasy.

"AAAAAHH!

Bella shrieked as the massive orgasm that had been building in the background erupted and shattered her being into millions of bursts of light that blew apart like a chrysanthemum skyrocket before she spun down into the darkness reserved for those who have been well and truly fucked.

She grinned at this assurance that not only was she an obedient sexual submissive, but that she was a submissive who was loved by her husband and master, and found Wally gently sponging her off with a warm facecloth and hot towel.

I do so love you, my very own Master, and I thank you, my dear, for the pleasure you just gave me, as she pulled his head down for a long, tender kiss.

"As I adore you, my lovely pet with a goddess' physique and an alley cat's morals. I consider myself lucky to have you as my wife, my pet, and my love. But if we don't tidy up and change, our visitors will start talking.

Would you kindly bring me my perfume from the bath, my love? "She murmured coyly, even as she took the facecloth from his hand and took over cleaning herself up.

The newlyweds took the elevator down to the ballroom where the reception was to be held, properly attired once more, with his medals in position and her lace veil left behind but with the coronet in place on her flame red hair. Wally put up with the seemingly endless photos in infinite combinations with good grace, and eventually everyone sat down to dinner.

So why were you a little late getting down here? she teased as Wally and Rose waltzed. Perhaps you two found something to do while you were getting ready. "

Let's just say that both sides of the historic battle of love declared victory.

"Ah. You speak French, my beloved daughter's husband? "

"A little, my dear... What should I say when I address you? "

However, given that you don't have a mother of your choosing, it would make me very happy if you called me "Maman."

"Very well... Maman."

After giving him a brief embrace and realizing the importance of that straightforward reply, she asked him, "How many languages do you speak, anyway?" to give them both a time to gather their composure.

"Portuguese is the only other language I genuinely know. I can muddle through in French, Spanish, and Cebuano well enough that I can usually communicate with a native speaker, but I don't think in those languages, if you get the difference.

After leading Wally to Admiral Corcoran, who was standing by a side door and appeared agitated, Rose began to respond but was stopped by her husband's gestures for her to follow him.

Wally arched an eyebrow at the Admiral, and his father-in-law continued, "Right now, Commander, my congratulations to you and your wife, and would both of you kindly attend me in this conference room right away."

To the displeasure of the bridesmaid he was squiring, Wally interrupted his wife while she was Samcing with Billy and said, "Sorry, Boots, but I need to borrow your sister for a minute."

Billy grinned, "Not a problem, I think my girlfriend would rather be out on the Samce floor than sulking at the table anyhow." Wally Samced Bella over to the side of the floor, where he took her hand and escorted her to the conference room.

"Wally, what's going on?

"I'm not sure, but it must be significant. They entered the room to find not only the Admiral and Rose waiting for them, but also Admiral Fulton, his wife, his personal assistant, and a naval pilot wearing khakis and an Officer of the Day armband.

"Commander, I regret to inform you and your wife of some awful news. While I am aware that you are on vacation, your orders have been modified. Wally received the document Admiral Fulton handed him and began reading as Bella watched over his shoulder.

"To: RADM Thomas Fulton, USN, Naval Surveillance Center

From: ComNavSurWarCen VADM Charles Pompeuse, USN

URGENT

1. I regret to inform you that on this date, CDR John Wilson perished in the crash of Southair Flight 803. Our office will handle notifying the next of kin in your absence. You will receive information copies of every activity.

2. It is essential that LCDR Wallace Jadens report right now to NavSurWarCen to take over command of the Project Sword crew given the

upcoming development of test basin models. Find the subject officer, explain the situation to him, and instruct him to obey verbal directions with written orders to follow as soon as possible.

I'm sorry, Wally, but your honeymoon with your wife will have to wait. After concluding talks with the West Coast's Special Warfare Combatant Craft community, Wilson was leaving Coronado after assuring them that the Swords could meet both the SEALs' and their standards. In fact, working with them in the same manner that you did with the Magsaysay in MinSamao because your mothership — swarm method has been successfully deployed in combat. The last obstacle we had to overcome before starting model testing was earning their trust.

You're going to be required at Carderock more than ever now that the computer modeling is finished, physical model construction will get underway on Monday, and test basin work will get underway as soon as feasible after that.

How quickly can you arrive there?

We'll leave tomorrow morning, Bella said as Wally turned to face her. "Even the Military wouldn't dare deny a bride her wedding night," she remarked. There's no need to tell the reception.

Wally did some mental calculation and stated, "I make the journey around 12 hours, Boss. It will simplify things if you can book us a room at the nearest guest house. The pod and our furniture were supposed to travel together and arrive in about a week.

Admiral Corcoran stepped in, saying, "Leave it to me; this is not the first permanent change of station we've dealt with. I'll organize shipping the pod to your new home with Rose. When an admiral phones to request a change in delivery dates, moving firms take their request seriously.

Admiral Fulton said, "And don't worry about a place to stay; your father told us about your house in Stafford, and Robin and I would be glad to put you up until it's ready.

CHAPTER 22

Wally remarked, "That being settled, let's rejoin the celebration. We've still the wedding cake to confront before Bella and I can reasonably go." They slid through the side entrance and into the ballroom, nodding to the flag officers and the Officer of the Day.

Bella slipped the Philippines Legion of Honor over her husband's necktie and added, "This day has been a long time coming."

Wally concurred, turning the medallion of one of the medals on his breast so the obverse was in the front. "There were moments when I wondered whether we'd ever make it, sweetie." After having to prove myself to the ring-knockers and the brainiacs, "first, taking charge of a team in shock after the death of its Project Manager at a vital juncture — "

She giggled, "Even the time you, with great flair, moved that engineer out with a stinging fitness report for patronizing Patch Flores after Patch came up with a better propulsion arrangement than he'd devised, in the hydrodynamics program at Rickover Hall. Things really came together after that, and you made it obvious that you didn't care where — or if — team members attended college as long as they had strong ideas that advanced the project.

"I thought Admiral Fulton was going to Samce a jig when he bet that Air Force general at the Edwards radar test range on how big a radar cross-section she'd have. The zoomie had his money on something the size of a lobster boat, and she turned out to have the cross-section of a 16 foot aluminum skiff. It wouldn't have, if Patch hadn't proved up the propulsion system before we got her out of the test basin."

When I said, "I christen thee USS Cutlass," and broke the champagne over her bow, the valves were opened to finish flooding the drydock and float her off the blocks, and they opened the dock gate and you took her out under her own power for the first time, I cried. Even if it was just a half mile jaunt to the fitting out basin, she looked beautiful underway. I don't think I've ever been as proud as I was on that day.

Wally put on her white leather gloves and pinned a big white hat that would have fit in the Royal Enclosure at Ascot at a jaunty angle to her hair. "You're sure you remember your role?" she questioned.

"What's to forget, Master? I stand there admiring you as the National Anthem is played, the Base Chaplain offers the invocation, you accept the plaque from the USS Cutlass Submarine Veterans Association recognizing the continuity of the name, Admiral Fulton makes a speech about the Cutlass being the latest and greatest, commanded by the most experienced littoral combat officer in the fleet, and reads the order putting her in commission, the Colors and tassels are presented, and the Not a thing. Let's meet the parents and start the performance.

As they entered, Wally's father and the Corcorans were already waiting there. Rose had gone ahead and arranged the cups and the coffee service. After greeting each other and giving them time to have their first cup of coffee, Bruce Jadens moved the conversation to a more serious subject.

The auction is tomorrow, and I can loan you the money to buy it outright against your stock holdings. Bella and I can go have a look at it while you're shaking the Cutlass down. I've found a house for you in Virginia Beach; it's not far from the base, and it's a sight better than any of those junior officer duplexes the Navy would assign you.

Wally remarked, "I would want. "And we have an advantage the house flippers don't have,"

Bella continued, "Boots taught Bella how to use an old fiber-optic camera rig that was just retired from some friends of his at Quantico. The lens is much larger than the current generation and the resolution isn't as good, but it's good enough to slip under a door or in a slightly open window and look inside.

Everyone nodded in agreement. "Once you get a new apartment, we can speak about getting this one rented, son. Additional money coming in never hurts."

When we arrived yesterday night, Rose said, "Wally, I was shocked you weren't home. You must have gotten back quite late."

Wally acknowledged, "I did. After practicing the commissioning ceremony, Patch Flores and I talked with the yard superintendent and the project managers for the Rapier, the Sabre, and the Scimitar. They had learned from our mistakes when building the Cutlass, and as a result, the Rapier is on schedule and the others are ahead of schedule.

In fact, for the construction program, the yard just purchased the historic USS Alamo back from the Brazilian Navy. It helps to having friends who occasionally tell you stuff; my Marinha do Brazil buddies felt I may be interested in what happened to our old sweetheart. When I found out they wanted to grow, I gave her the yard. Her well deck is large enough to allow the shipyard to build two Cutlasses side by side and under cover, but the Brazilians are retiring her since she is too worn out for continued ocean duty. They will gain a lot more office and storage space as a bonus and it will be cheaper and faster to purchase an old LSD than to build new drydocks. The Sword program will be expedited, and it is a good bargain all around.

"Ha-hmm," said Admiral Corcoran, clearing his throat. Wally smiled and took it, noting that it was far too light to be cookies or pastry. He opened it and his eyes widened. It contained an officer's cap with the single row of oak leaves on the brim that is worn by Navy captains and commanders. It was nowhere near new; Admiral Corcoran had clearly worn it prior to becoming a flag officer.

"You know I should be out on the flight line, not stuck behind a desk at the Pentagon. Considering that I spend my days dealing with career rear echelon motherfuckers, politicians, and lobbyists, there are moments when I question whether gaining another star is worthwhile. But it does provide me an opportunity to engage in some political maneuvering.

CHAPTER 23

As the new ships of her class are commissioned, they will join you at Little Creek as part of Patrol Craft Squadron One's rear echelon, training Riverine Squadron 1 in your mothership - piranha tactics. By next year, when we have enough of them, they will be organized into a division, which will be the foundation of Patrol Craft Squadron Two.

"Commanders lead their divisions — "
Which leads us to this," said Rose, handing him a box the size of a pen and pencil set. When Wally opened it, he saw a pair of three-stripe shoulder boards, the bullion in the stripes aged and tainted by salt air to the hue of ancient gold.
"The head of the Bureau of Personnel is now John's roommate from Annapolis. The Navy anticipates having four Patrol Craft Littorals in

service and four more on the way by the end of the next year, as evidenced by the commander's list he presented to him. Your name will be on that list, and you will be given leadership of the first PCL division, so long as you don't tread on your crank between now and then.

The Admiral interjected, saying, "But don't expect to have it for long. I've planned to send you to the Navy War College at Newport on the lengthy course when you have been promoted. You'll be qualified for any surface ship or shore command in the Navy once you do that, but knowing you, I anticipate you'll want to get back out on the water. The first twelve PCLs will be operational by then, if those dimwits on the Hill don't reduce our budget, and the second flight of Cutlasses will be under construction. You are our most seasoned brown water officer, and the Brown Water Navy will require squadron commanders.

The Navy expects a lot more service from you and your Gator Navy, my dear. You are more qualified than anybody I know to do it. I'm really happy for you! Everyone in the room was stunned by Bella's open-mouthed kiss on him, with the exception of Rose, whose eyes twinkled with restrained amusement.

Charge your glasses, or coffee cups, as the Admiral said. After everyone had coffee in their cups, he hoisted his own and proclaimed, "Here's to the USS Cutlass, her loyal crew, and her intrepid commander." May their service bring honor to the Navy!"

THE END

Printed in June 2023
by Rotomail Italia S.p.A., Vignate (MI) - Italy